# A HIRED BLADE

AN
EVERLANDS CYCLE
NOVELLA

## J.C. RYCROFT

BATTLEWARRIOR
PRESS

Copyright © JC Rycroft 2022

First ebook edition December 2022

First print edition February 2023

Cover by Fay Lane

Illustrations by Myfanwy Cadwallader

Developmental editing by Cameron Montague Taylor

of The AuthorShip Publishing and Editorial Services

Copy and line editing by Rachelle Wright of R. A. Wright Editing

Proofreading by Nay of That Grammar Gal

Ebook ISBN: 978-0-6456228-0-5

Print ISBN: 978-0-6456228-1-2

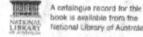 A catalogue record for this book is available from the National Library of Australia

A BattleWarrior Press book

First published in Australia in 2023 by BattleWarrior Press

Ebook first published in 2022 by BattleWarrior Press

Visit the author's website at www.JCRycroft.com

For the Rogue Writers—
for their gentleness, encouragement, and insight.
And for not hating me for the end of this book (much!).

# Author Note

This novella is not all puppies and sunshine, I'm afraid, and there's some naughty language, dark events, and explicit content.

For a full content note (including a comprehensive set of trigger warnings), which I'd encourage you to check if you're wondering 'what exactly do they mean by dark, though?', please flick to the very last page of the book, or visit this novella's online home at https://jcrycroft.com/a-hired-blade

# AUTHOR'S NOTE

# CHAPTER ONE

I grin as I bound up the stairs, skipping every second step, and stride across the porch into the Wrestler's Wrangle. My skirts shift around my legs and my sword juts above my shoulder, drawing a couple gazes. Few women in Rescalin carry blades so openly, but I'm a traveling sellsword, so my appearance is half how I announce my wares.

The Wrestler's Wrangle lies in Calor, one of the satellite towns around Pastira, the capital of Rescalin. Much of the less formal parts of the business of the capital take place here. I wonder if that's what Karina called me here for.

This pub has gotta be my favorite place to raise a glass in the whole country. It's clean, the beer is good, and the lanterns hung from the ceiling cast warm light over golden-brown wood. Comfy. And there's Karina.

I have fond if alcohol-fuzzed memories of Karina and her crew raising sloshing cups with me and Petrus at the conclusion of another long caravan. That was the last run, or maybe the one before. I frown. That one had taken us from a harbor on the northern coast through grassy plains, across hills, and down through scrubby bush that hems in the sands of the Great Red Desert. I hope she's not proposing that same route in reverse. It'd been a good trip, but I'm not sure how it'd go without Petrus.

"Des!" Karina's marketplace-practiced bellow cuts through the roaring burble of chatter and laughter inside. I scan the edge of the room until I spot her, black corkscrew coils bouncing around her face. She leans out one of the short rows of booths—the ones designed for business of one kind or another. In the next one along, a woman in clothing loose enough to be almost falling off her is clambering in to seat herself alongside a brawny man who can't take his eyes off her breasts.

I slide myself into Karina's booth and meet her dark, dancing eyes. Tiny silver mirrors decorate her burgundy blouse and scatter light over her bronze face. As I expect, her bright grin sets me smiling.

"It's good to see you, my friend." She grips my arm in greeting, her muscles almost matching mine. I earned my strength through swordplay, while hers was built tossing bolts of cloth and carpets in and out of wagons. Karina and her sister, Shameela, run one of the leading textile merchant companies in Rescalin. Shameela handles the office and the warehouses in Pastira, while Karina tends to be out gathering up goods or managing market stalls. "I feel like it's been an age."

"Not so very long," I counter. "What was it, only a half a cycle since Petrus and I took you from Tyrasene to Pastira?"

Her smile shifts to a little coquettish, and I almost double-take. "Yes, but I'm talking of how it's felt." Gods, is Karina flirting with me? "Anyway, where's that lad?"

The question is expected. Even so, it makes my smile stutter. "Petrus and I have parted company."

"For truth?" Her brows rise, shock abrading the scabbed wound of our parting. "I thought you'd... well, I didn't expect that, is all."

I manage a smile, but it's a bit tight round the edges. I can feel it. Not my best play. "I didn't neither, really."

I can see her working through whether to ask about it. "Well, I won't pry," she says, "but I won't pretend I'm not curious. I'm sorry, though. I know you two were like family."

The sympathy is more than I've had since Petrus stormed out on me four months ago. Granted, I've been traveling solo and earning money from folks who hadn't known the two of us since. Karina's compassion makes my nose prickle with the threat of tears. It's true. We'd been family for so long.

At sixteen, I joined the players' troupe Petrus traveled with. It hadn't been him I was following, though. I'd fallen head over heels for Liv—gorgeous, green-eyed, ebony-haired Liv—and my whole little village had turned against me and run me out. The head of the troupe had agreed to keep me on, mostly to satisfy Liv. She usually gets her way.

Petrus and I had been friends almost from the beginning, and it was he who helped me leave the troupe when I could no longer bear Liv's hot-and-cold—her cruelty and her love. It was he who helped me conceal my sex at Shambullion's Swordsman's School, and who practiced with me 'til we left with skills we could put to earning. Then we traveled nigh on three years together, taking mercenary contracts for protection or border skirmishes and occasionally tripping to outlaw territory when work was thin.

But the truth had finally come out. The memory of that night makes me bite the inside of my lip, the physical pain preferable to the emotional. He'd been in a helpless fury I'd never seen on him before. The words are forever etched into my mind, as is the agony carved into his face, the way his eyes were lit with pain and anger. "I've been in love with you for five years. Five fucking years, Des! I helped you leave! I helped you build a life after Picton's. I've been at your side, faithful as she could *never* be. And now, even now, three years since you've seen that black-haired bitch, she's all you talk about!"

He'd flipped a table and stalked out before I could find the words to respond, not that I had much to say. When my heart had eased its racing, I realized that as anger had earned my freedom from Liv, such as it was, Petrus needed his rage in order to let me go. As bad as I felt for not seeing his love had turned romantic, I could never return his feelings. Petrus is handsome—very much so; he'd never lacked for attention—but I couldn't. I sleep with men when they catch my eye, but it never occurred to me to sleep with Petrus. Better to let him go, as much as it broke my heart.

Karina's dark hand coils in over the top of my interlaced two, easing my knuckles away from white. I glance up, almost in shock she's there. The memory of that night is still so intense it's hard to let it go. I meet her eyes, feeling half-ashamed of the tears I know are gilding my own. "I'm so sorry, Des," she says, and the compassion in her face makes me gasp in a breath against the sob that wants out.

"I'm alright," I lie, voice quavering.

"You will be." Her gaze is warm on mine, and with a little huff of embarrassment, I pull a hand free to dash tears from my face.

"I will be," I repeat, "but this is hardly why you called me here."

"No." Karina sits back and takes a deep breath. "Alright, I can talk at business if you need." She meets my eyes. "We need a protection crew. The same run as last time. From here to Tyrasene and back again. There's a cargo coming in from Ascelin, and we've bought in on more than half of it. We need to get it back to the capital by the turn to summer. And we're carrying goods from here, ready to be taken to Aredoma in Ascelin. They like our clothes there, and we like their linens."

She levels her gaze at me thoughtfully. "You and Petrus were the perfect leads last time. Kept the other hires in line, away from excessive drink or brawling with locals where we had to stop. And you know how we are about keeping good relationships all over. Plus, those two bandit attacks came to nothing but a few bruises in the end, and that's what we pay for, right?"

I lick my lips. "Yeah. Look, you know you and the rest of the company are a dream to work for, and I'd never want to turn you down when you need us—need me—but without Petrus..."

Karina's dark gaze glimmers with amusement. "Is this your new sales pitch, Des? It needs some work."

I laugh, then settle back against the wall of the booth with a sigh. "Blessed heaven, to think I'd thought that Petrus was the brawn and me the brains of the operation! I need a beer."

I flag down a passing waitress with a basket of dirty glasses braced on her hip and place my order, then turn back to Karina. "Most of the crew we hired last time are elsewhere right now. I heard Pink was down on the border with Kebble, working for the king..."

I rumble through a list of the crew Petrus and I had brought on last time. One lost a leg recently; another was signed up to a mercenary company. There was only one I could think of as possibly free to join up with us. Karina gives me a sardonic look as I trail off. She says nothing for a long moment, but her eyes go from assessing to warm.

"Maybe your sales pitch isn't so very terrible," she says, with a grin. She leans forward, her blouse falling open to reveal the top of her impressive cleavage. Curves for days. "We need you, Des. Surely you know other mercenaries you could hire?"

I rest back and take a long draft to settle my nerves. "I know them sure enough. Some I even like. But they're, well..." I'm a good enough mercenary and can hold my own amongst a team, but I'm not a leader. Gods, I'm a country kid with only a couple years behind me.

"Please, Des." She sighs. "We've pinned too much of our capital to this trip." Her coils bounce again as she shakes her head. "That's Shameela's talk. Sorry. We've spent too much money not to get the payoff. We've dealt with the Ascelese before. We *must* be there on time or we lose our deposit, as well as all the promises we have riding on us getting that fabric. We can't wait around testing a new merc with minor journeys to see if they're trustworthy. We have to move." She's pleading now.

I turn it over in my head. I can't do what's she's asking. I'm not a strong enough fighter—not yet, anyway—but I could do with some coin. It's been tougher to find work since Petrus left, and Karina's easy to work for. It'd be a dream job, except I can't lead. I'm greener'n grass, as so many mercs have told me. But I can't just walk away either. I take another draft of beer, pondering.

Best solution would be if someone else who knows me—some other merc who knows his way around leadership—could take this job. Might even learn from him, whoever it winds up being. I narrow my eyes as a thought strikes. "I can think of one possible way," I admit.

Karina cocks her head, meeting my gaze as a slow smile unfurls on her face, and my breath goes short. When she speaks, her voice is husky with a promise I dare not contemplate.

"I'm all ears."

# CHAPTER TWO

I've almost won the negotiations, but I don't like the doubt gnawing at my innards. A pragmatic decision, I remind myself. A way to make it work. To help Karina out and get me some coin. It's the right call—works for everyone. But still, it gnaws.

Opposite me, the captain resembles a weathered wooden carving in ruddy browns and black, the many rows of tanned wrinkles akin to the wood grain. His wavy hair is midnight threaded with silver, greasy, and bound back tight in a tie at his nape except for the few strands that fall across his weathered face. His dark eyes are sunk amongst crow's feet, and they're cunning enough to have kept me cautious for our whole acquaintance.

I've worked with him before, mostly on campaigns for the Crown. He can lead men; I've seen it. He was the obvious choice of all of those I know. And, as luck had it, he wasn't too far from the capital. I'd ridden out after shaking hands over a deal with Karina and found him barely two days away. He was hungover but prepared to talk, thankfully.

"Let's be clear now, though, Des. You might be the one hiring us all on, but I'm in charge." His voice is like gravel, as always. "You might know this client, but I'm not having you try and lead some kind of mutiny against me."

I laugh, the sound easy, belying the doubts in my gut. "Cap, the last thing I want is to be in charge. I'm weary. It's been a tough year. I just want to be along—pulling my weight, of course, but not more than that. You know I'll do that much. You don't need to worry."

He drinks long from his enormous tankard, draining it down. A boy grabs the empty glass from in front of him, and he nods at the lad's wordless question. With narrowed eyes, he assesses me again, then settles back, as if reaching a conclusion. "I always thought Petrus was in charge, even though he claimed you was both the bosses." A full tankard plunks down in front of him.

My smile doesn't crack. Cap's watching me close. I can tell he's testing me. I set aside my pride and shrug a little. "Petrus's dreams, not mine. I want to get along, get the job done. Need someone in charge who knows what they're doing." It burns a little, saying the words.

He nods, satisfied. "Alrighty. You're well enough with the blade, so you'll be a good one on the crew. But you keep outta my way, let me choose the rest of the men, don't fuck any of those I choose. You can do that, you got yourself a deal. Fifteen golds and twenty silvers for me, and I'm gonna need ten golds and ten for each of the rest of the crew. A third up front, a third at Tyrasene, and a third on completion."

It's within the parameters Karina and I discussed. It's what we planned. It's success. I ignore the curl in my gut, nod with a deal more certainty than I'm feeling, and stick my hand out. It's hard not to regret Petrus's departure right this second. "Good to have you aboard, Cap. We head out from Pastira in a five day, so we'll need to get on finding ourselves a crew."

"Good to be working with you, Des. Don't worry. I've done this route a dozen times, and I know some rogues who'll be perfect for this kind of job. As luck has it, they're all here in Kreshell. We'll be there." His eyes almost disappear into the crinkles as he grins, showing me teeth gone blackened and brown. He grips my hand tight—too tight, really. The kind of grip I've learned is merc code for testing who's stronger. I let him have it.

I sigh and shift awkwardly on the hard wooden bench, sat with my back exposed to the rest of the drunken crowd. It's a dark tav, this one, in the middle of Pastira, and I can't help but be a little edgy.

The new crew are hardly offering the most scintillating conversation. Not that mercs ever do. I miss Petrus. We could exchange a glance and know it was a placeholder for the riotous laughter we'd share in private. Somehow, it'd made all the difference.

I catch the captain assessing me, and I grin, hoist the tankard high, and offer a nod. He gives me an ugly smirk—the man's not capable of otherwise—and a nod back. Gods. I hate the get-to-know-you bit of forming a crew. It always seemed so much easier for Petrus.

There's six of us total. Cap. Myself. Pulldark, graying and carrying a notched, curved blade. Rizzen, with slender brown eyes and clever fingers, and a dizzying array of weaponry strapped about his person. Jamil, locs tied back in a green cloth and with a gaze that seems not to miss a beat. And Bols, wielding both a double-headed axe and the shoulders to make it work, off getting yet another drink from the bar.

He's returned. Bols sways into me, and I shove back jovially with my shoulder, but he double-takes at the sight of me beside him. "Sure this one's gonna pull her weight, Cap?" His sally is met with ribald laughter. I've not worked with any of them before, but Bols, stolid and red-faced, is clearly one to keep an eye on.

I roll my eyes. Every damn time. So I pull out the same performance, perfected over an age, it feels like. "I could pull your weight as well as my own, brother," I say, and the cluster around us hoots and whistles. They eat this shit up.

"You challenging me?" he asks, turning toward me so I can better appreciate how difficult it is for him to fit alongside others on a bench.

"I could, but I feel it's more you're the one doing the challenging... of the captain's assessment, tell ya true." It's said not too quietly, and I sip at my beer while his spluttering spirals up. "After all, he added me to this crew. Cap? Want me to defend your honor? Just say the word."

Now Cap's spluttering. In a moment, the two roar at one another, until Bols recollects Cap will be the one to pay us come the end of this gig and finds a way back from getting himself ditched from the team. The three others in our little crew watch on, hoping for a fight. I smile mildly at Cap, and his eyes narrow.

"What time do we move out tomorrow, Cap?" I ask, knowing I'm gonna need to not have a hangover tomorrow so I can deal with Bols and his ego.

"Got someplace you need to be, Des?" Cap asks, and he casts a wink around.

"Thought I might visit the baths, make myself a bit less unpleasant to be around." It doesn't matter that I'm self-deprecating, there's yet more hoots. Gods. I need to get out of this tav. Drunken mercs can be painful. "Plus, didn't you say it was an early start?"

"That I did, that I did," Cap says, getting serious. "Leastways, that's what the client wants. But, y'know, I reckon we can make up the time."

I sigh and push myself to stand. Between Petrus and me, it used to be we could find a gracious out from these kinds of team-building exercises, but I'm still working on an exit that's foolproof. And now I've got the extra weight of trying to keep the captain to Karina's schedule. Fabulous. "Well, I'll meet you at the caravan. I'll be there a half hour before we're meant to leave—at the half bell after seven. Karina will have a crew loading up, but there's more likely to be bonuses in it for those who show themselves willing to do extra."

Cap narrows deep-set, dark eyes at me, and I smile as blandly as I can manage. "Enjoy your drinks, confreres." I raise my hand in farewell.

"Enjoy your soap," Cap jeers behind me.

"Oh, I intend to!" I throw over my shoulder, grinning fit to bust. The moment I turn around, I lose the expression. I miss traveling with Petrus—or even without him—when I didn't have to perform anywhere near as much as this crew are gonna need.

# CHAPTER THREE

"Gorgeous morning, isn't it?" Wens, one of Karina's crew, greets me with a yell from where he's busy tossing chests into a wagon, the last in a line of over six. Four caravans sit to one side. It's on the long side, the convoy, and it likely means there's going to be more strangers to get to know beyond the four drunkards Cap's signed up for our protection crew. The sun soaks into my shoulders, and I wriggle at the warmth. "Karina's at the front with Shameela."

I grin and nod, leading Liza, my horse, toward him. Her ears prick forward at the possibility of new companions. Since Petrus left—taking his horse, Ebony, with him—Liza's been lonely too. "And Issian and Morwell?"

"Runnin' around here somewhere. You know how Karina gets when we're headin' out." Wens's grin is broad. He loves being on the move. "You can hook Liza to this wagon if you like. She's such a lovely beast!" He throws himself from the wagon tray down to the ground and hurries over to stroke Liza's nose. She leans into the caress, and I almost laugh at her as I tie the reins to the wagon. "Oh, and Besta's joining us this time, did you know?"

I laugh. "Oh, blessed heavens. I'm not sure we have protection enough to compensate for that lad's enthusiasm."

Besta is Karina's son, cherished by all and about as lively and cheerful as a kid can be. I have no doubt the caravan will wind up cursing out his presence and feeling grateful for his singing and smile in equal measure.

I make my way down the long line of wagons and caravans as the bell for half seven rings. Cap should be here already. It's his first workday, by the gods.

At the front of the line of wagons, I find Karina, arms crossed and talking to Shameela, who is turned half away from me and gesturing at the warehouse. Karina catches sight of me before her sister, and the smile that slowly blossoms across her face is beyond satisfied.

I grin bemusedly at her, taken aback. If I'd gotten that look across a bar, I'd have known I wasn't going lonely that night, but it's confusing to confront it in the stark light of day. It makes me straighten my clothes to be sure I'm decent.

Shameela catches sight of her sister's gaze and turns to see what she's smiling at just as I come within earshot.

"... priorities!"

"I am used to managing multiple demands," Karina says, not taking her eyes from me, her voice so calm it's salacious.

I can't help the flush I know cascades down my face, but I ignore it as much as I can and hold my hand out to Shameela. "Excellent to see you again, Shameela. You're looking well."

It's true. Shameela is well-dressed, in silks tailored into fashion that somehow is flattering and unusual at the same time, with earrings that dangle almost to her shoulders and her hair wrapped into bantu knots. Impractical, but she can do that here in the capital. She gives me a look caught between amusement and frustration. "Thank you, Des, you're too kind. You look well too, though Karina told me about Petrus. I'm sorry to hear it."

The sympathy here is genuine, though Shameela knew Petrus and I less well. And, once again, I have to swallow back the sting before I nod my thanks. "I don't mind traveling solo," I say. "So few others to please."

This draws a laugh from Shameela, and she sends a significant look to Karina. "Ah, the dream," she remarks sardonically.

Karina laughs too, and a moment later, Besta flies at speed out of the ware-house and almost runs into Shameela. She steps back to avoid him crashing into her but extends her arms to catch him.

"Besta! Steady on or you'll scare the horses, and we cannot afford that in this courtyard. Far too full." Karina's tone is severe.

"Sorry, Mama." He's perfected his performance of chastened since I've seen him last, but he holds it for too short a period to be totally convincing. "Issian says he'll let me take the reins on the wagon pulled by Jester and Kip!"

Karina opens her mouth, the frown already dawning on her face. "Now, now," comes Issian's booming voice, his slender form loping into view out of the shadows of the warehouse. "I said at some point in this journey I'm sure I'll be forced to hand a wagon over to you, but I'd only trust you at the reins with Jester and Kip."

I grin. "Hasn't Jester done this trip so many times you set him in the right direction and he'll practically take himself?"

Besta laughs along with the rest of us but pouts a little. "He did promise."

Karina cuddles her son in against her soft belly for a moment. "I've already discussed it with Issian. The plan is you'll be slowly trained in guiding the horses and we'll see how that goes. I have no doubt by the time we reach Tyrasene you'll be leading the wagons through the city. But that's a good six, eight weeks from now."

Besta's eyes light up, though Issian shakes his head at Karina. Shameela laughs at his disapproval and shrugs. "Well, you're the head of this caravan now, Karina. You decide what goes. Just make sure everyone understands that."

"I feel sure that Issian, Wens, Morwell, and Des know how it works, sis," Karina says comfortably. "And Besta should too…"

I smile a little, warmth blossoming in my chest at being included in the close-knit group. Cap'll have to get it as well. That's my real job here—making sure this arrangement works for Karina and Shameela.

As if my thought produced him out of nowhere, Cap strides scowling into the courtyard, Rizzen and Jamil flanking him while Bols and Pulldark dawdle behind. The two at the back have hands full of food they're scoffing as they walk.

I realize with narrowed eyes that the three at the front are pasty-pale in all the various shades of their skin. They're striding out ahead of the smell of the food, and it makes my mouth tighten when I see Jamil's body jerk in the telltale way of a suppressed gag. Must've been a good night.

But Cap, at the front, looks the least worse for wear, and he meets my eyes with that same cunning gleam. "Ms. Shelta? Or shall I say Mses. Sheltas, if I don't mistake my guess?" It's almost charming as he holds his hand out first to Shameela, then to Karina—or it would be but for his ugly grin.

"Shameela, Karina, this is Cap, head of security for the caravan," I say formally, mostly for the benefit of those around us.

The two women nod and shake his hand, murmuring niceties. "We're keen to be underway, Cap," Karina says briskly as soon as the greetings are done. "We'd hoped to beat the half-seven bell, but we're playing catch-up now."

There's a reprimand in there, and it's not deeply buried, but Cap ignores it entirely. "Of course, ma'am. Let's be on our way. I'll set one of my crew to the back of every second caravan or so, keep the cargo secure as we head through the city. We can manage introductions over camp setup tonight."

"Thanks," Karina says, a little terse. She didn't get the apology she was after.

"Off to be crew," I murmur as Cap moves out of earshot, trailed by Issian. "Lovely to see you again, Shameela, and we'll see you again soon. I promise I'll keep your family safe."

Shameela's expression softens as she turns to me. "Thank you, Des. I always worry, and Karina always tells me I'm ridiculous. But thank you. And keep yourself safe too. You're pretty close to family, you know."

The warmth in her quick hug and in her words makes me flush again, and I swallow. Gods, this family! Generous to the end. But something has happened behind my back, and as we release the embrace, Shameela and Karina are already laughing about something I don't understand. I leave them to it, with a brisk nod to Karina and Besta. As I turn to trail after Cap, Pulldark vomits against a wall.

# CHAPTER FOUR

I settle against the back of the wagon, my legs dangling off as it lurches forward. I'm giving Liza a break from my weight and enjoying the change of pace. Wens is driving the next horse in our snaking caravan, and we're exchanging relaxed banter. Besta races past, yelling at the top of his lungs to his mother and making the horses shift uneasily. I grin and shake my head.

"Des." Cap nods as he strides past, heading for the front of the caravan. He's carrying a skin, and I nearly ask whether it's wine. Surely not. I've had a riding crop taken to my ass for less from other leaders. Then he takes a swallow and there's no mistaking it. Wine. On the job. It's like Petrus is here with me, shaking his head and horrified.

"Cap," I reply. I hesitate over commenting on the wine, but he's gone before I can find words. What would I even say? He's the boss.

It turns out the captain has done this trip a fair few times, and he'd know it backward. He's done well enough the past few days, but we're still in the safer part of the journey, close by Pastira and the surrounding towns. It's once we wind up meandering alongside the desert that I'll really start to worry. That's when the brigands usually show up.

I watch 'til he moves out of view, kicking my heels against the wagon in a regular rhythm. Besta reappears, Karina smiling behind him, and bounces up onto the wagon beside me. "I like that beat!" His brown eyes are wide with delight. He is loving this trip, and it's hard not to catch his joy.

"This one?" I ask, and add a double tap.

He grins at me and pounds a closed fist on the side of the wagon he can reach. "Sounds like..."

"'Carmeline'?" Karina asks, and with a little jump, she's up alongside me, the length of her thigh pressed to mine. "Alright, kid, you keep that beat, I'll sing the melody, and you can harmonize when you work out how to."

It turns out "Carmeline" is the kind of bawdy song popular in taverns from Pastira to Hathway. It's a tale of a woman and the several men she fools into becoming her lovers at the same time, without their knowledge—sometimes physically. The impossibility of the story keeps me giggling, and Karina's wicked gaze dancing from Besta's grinning face to mine makes me feel all kinds of warm.

After a moment, Wens picks up the harmony from the driver's seat of the wagon trailing ours, and I hear Issian's clear tenor rise from the front. I grin in delight, and in a breathless moment between verses, Karina leans against me. "C'mon, Des, you must know the song! Join me!"

I choke on the first few notes, but soon enough, I'm singing along with her, despite barely remembering the words. I venture into harmony at one point—it's an almost-forgotten skill from when I was amongst Picton's troupe—and am rewarded with a dazzling, delighted smile from Karina. Besta's soprano tones meld with my own alto.

We finish together on a loud "hey!" that resounds up and down the caravan, and then Karina collapses against me, chuckling, and I find my arm around her as I laugh too. "I reckon we could find ourselves a side gig in performing." Wens has to raise his voice to be heard over our laughter.

I groan loudly, grinning. "Oh gods, I promised myself I'd never pick it back up!"

Karina gives me a curious look. "You mean you used to be a player? I never knew that."

"It's how Petrus and I met," I explain. "We were in the same troupe."

"Does that mean you know how to juggle?" Besta interrupts, and I'm almost glad. Karina's gaze has grown too intense for my comfort. "And walk a tightrope?"

I laugh. "Well... it's been a while, and tightropes were never my thing, but I can manage the juggle, at least for a bit. And I did have some tumbling, though my main role was being the solid foundation at the bottom of a pyramid."

A memory of Liv flits through my mind. She'd climbed up my body until she was standing on my shoulders, about to jump across to be caught by Umina. Picton was roaring at us both to hurry the fuck up. "Look up," she'd insisted, standing above me, and when I did, I caught an eyeful. She'd had no underwear on. "Just a sneaky preview of tonight's performance," she'd told me, her voice low and resonant with promise. I still remember, even now, the flush of desire that had cascaded through my body.

I shake the memory free, shoving back at the ache of hatred thinking of Liv always brings on. Liv is a long, long, long way away, no doubt, and not just physically. I don't want her anywhere near me.

Karina, on the other hand, is right here, smiling at me and raising an expectant brow while Besta yanks on my sleeve. They've been waiting on an answer, and I don't even know the question. Fucking Liv. Karina saves me. "Well, will you throw some plums for us, Des?"

I grin. "So long as we don't mind a few bruises, sure."

Besta tosses himself off the back of the wagon with a delighted cackle and runs to find the bag of the small fruit we purchased yesterday. "Thank you for indulging him," Karina says. "I'd been worried he might be a bit... bored, you know? Amongst so many adults. But you're great with him."

I meet her gaze. "Besta's a lot of fun," I say honestly. "And it's at least half me indulging myself, you know."

Karina's smile shifts to being a pleased mama for a moment, then to something a little naughtier. "Indulge away, Des. I've always wondered what that would look like."

I swallow, disappearing in the dark pools of her eyes, desperately trying to find a response. Eventually, I ask, "You did?"

Karina looks away, and it's almost shy. "I'd always assumed... well, I shouldn't have, I know, but Petrus was always around, and always, well... always looking like he does. I'm not interested in men, really, but even I could appreciate a good-looking man." She's not meeting my eyes, and it's so unlike her I feel almost charmed by her sudden shyness.

"He's very handsome," I say flatly, "and he knows it. He also knows women know it."

"But not you?" The curious gaze flashes to my face and then away again.

I lean back on my hands, conscious again of the length of her thigh warm against mine. The tangle between us unfurls something in my gut, and stretching against it feels good. "Not me. It's... well, it's why we parted. I had no idea..."

"That he loved you?" The words are blunt enough to make me wince. Karina's chuckle at my reaction is low. "Seriously, Des?" She shook her head. "I don't know how you can be that smart and that oblivious at the same time."

I open my mouth to reply but close it again almost at once.

"Well..." Besta's voice can be heard in the distance, and I'm almost relieved this line of conversation is about to shift. "In case the obliviousness extends further..." She sends me a quick grin and then can't meet my eyes again. "...you're only misreading what I'm seeking if you think it's naught but what you're being paid for." She pushes herself off the back of the wagon and saunters away.

It's deliberately convoluted. There's enough in my head for it to take me a moment to decode, and by then she's telling Besta not to waste all the plums on a juggling display before disappearing back up the caravan. I'm thankful as it means she misses my flush. I inhale, letting myself enjoy the sensation of this slow uncurling. A moment later, her son is bouncing up onto the seat beside me, begging me to show him my skills.

I turn to him with a grin. "Ready? Now, did you just want a display, or do you want to learn?"

His eyes get even bigger. "Learn? You could teach me?"

I shrug and pick three plums out of the paper bag. "Well, I can try!" I toss the three into the air, beginning the juggle. "I remember the woman who taught me. Umina, she was called, and she told me she'd never seen such a terrible student in all her life." I scoop up another four plums in a rhythm, adding them into the toss. "But I don't know. I feel like I got there in the end, what do you think?"

Besta's mouth is a round *O* of amazement and approval, and I grin. The wagon chooses that moment to hit a pothole, and we jerk out of alignment with my tossed plums. They cascade around us, one landing with a squishy wet sound on the wagon seat itself.

"Oops!" We say the word in unison, and I add, "Don't tell your mother!"

# CHAPTER FIVE

We roll into Enishae before sunset on the fifth day. It's a small village by the edge of the Great Red Desert, and behind the last building, the low scrub gives way to ocher rock and silver-gray bushes that would barely brush my knees. Enishae relies on the road for most of its income, so the tavern folk are solicitous and welcoming, but Karina is cautious. In these small towns, caravans like ours are sustenance for both the legitimate and illegitimate trades.

It takes a while to get all the caravans and wagons into their places. Cap sets a guard over the wagons that spill out of the tavern courtyard and into the field alongside, and doles out the watches through the night to pairs. I luck out with the midnight-to-four shift with Jamil, giving me no time for proper sleep.

I eat dinner alongside Besta and Karina on the long bench seats pulled up to scungy tables inside. Issian, Wens, and Morwell seat themselves between the three of us and the rest of the mercenaries, who are already well on their way to sloshed. Rizzen and Pulldark are on watch already. The meal is good, solid fare with no surprises, and I'm ready for an early night so I can manage my watch when the time comes.

A rap at my door rouses me, and I could swear it's early. But Bols, already halfway down the hall, weaving like a prizefighter, calls over his shoulder, "You're on." I guess it's my watch.

I pull on my proper clothes, sword in its harness, bow and quiver, and my rarely used cloak. Sharpening kit in hand, I knock gently on Jamil's door. "I'm heading down. See you when you get there," I say.

The chill bites as soon as I open the door to outside, and I whisk the cloak around my shoulders, rearranging the fabric around the jutting hilt of my sword. Jamil catches up with me. "Coolish, ain't it?" I say, with a grin.

"Mpf," he replies, scooping his locs back into their green cloth. Charming. Not a midnight-to-four kind of person, clearly.

We trot together across the courtyard and out into the field, where the wagons full of precious cloth lie. There're two tall stumps pulled up to a small fireplace. The fire will stop us stiffening up from the cold, but it sinks the shadows further out into blackness. Jamil claims his stump while I roll another lumpy log onto the dimming fire. I kick two empty bottles away from my seat.

It takes a while before Jamil rouses enough to manage words, but he does. "You knew Karina and her sister from before, right?"

I nod, running my sharpening stone against the blade of my second-favorite dagger. "I did. I've done this run before."

"Huh," he says. "And has it been smooth?"

I raise a shoulder. "Smoothish. I think last time there were two attempts on us?"

"I've never done a caravan before," he says. "Generally, I've stuck to guarding stuff in cities or taking a contract with the Crown."

"That how you know Cap?"

He nods. "Saved my life, he did. Three years back or so, I reckon. Cavalry coming in hard, and both my blades trapped in some dead man's spine. He blocked the rider's axe. Would've been my head."

"He's a good man to have at your back in a fight," I agree. "I met him doing Crown work too."

"You an' whatshisname? Petron?"

"Petrus," I say, my heart sinking a little. Just what I need—stories about Petrus and me circulating amongst the crew.

Something prods at my consciousness, like a sound I haven't quite heard. "You hear that?" I say in a low voice. I turn my ears away from the fireplace and its crackling and concentrate, closing my eyes to focus.

Jamil is an old enough hand at this kind of work that he doesn't dismiss me. He narrows his eyes, turning toward the woods. A moment later, he stands, reaches for his twin swords, and draws them slowly and quietly together. "Something's out there," he says, soft as soft. "You got a bow?"

Archery isn't my strength—my sword's my best weapon—but I quickly string the bow I have and hook the quiver I'd had leaning against the stump to my hip. I draw an arrow tight and sight along the shaft, turning to scan the opposite side of the clearing to where Jamil's eyes remain pinned.

I step away from the fire, and as my eyes adjust, I can make out movement among the bushes. I loose my arrow without hesitation and scoop another from my thigh, drawing again immediately. It strikes nothing, but the stillness seems deeper somehow, like someone's taken the warning. "Shall we call for the others?" I say.

"Mpf," comes Jamil's negative. "Let's be sure first."

As if that were the signal, three shapes lunge out of the shadows I'm gazing into. I release at the movement and catch up another arrow, loosing it too. One strikes, and I hear it—hear the body land hard, the gasp of pain mixed with the huffed-out breath of collision.

"Jamil?" I cry urgently, not daring to spin around as I drop my bow and draw my sword. Three men, bearded and bearing rough straight swords, are coming right at me. They're not yelling. They know if the tavern turns out they haven't a hope.

Behind me, closer than I expected, Jamil bellows toward the tavern, but there's no response.

"We need backup," he says grimly. "There's more out there than just this lot."

I parry and cut across the first fighter's neck, and he falls, spurting blood. There's warmth against my back for a split second, then I'm forced to step forward and between the two remaining attackers, slashing one side while dodging the other, then spinning to meet the blade again. My sword screeches as Jamil steps in to cut down the first. I disengage and cut around, carving into the third attacker's side. Blood spurts, and he falls heavy to the ground.

As if his words have magicked them out of the ether, four more men appear from the trees on the far side of the fire. My heart bounds into my throat at the sight. How the fuck are we going to call the others down now? Jamil roars again, and my howl joins his as we set ourselves up on either side of the flames, but there's no response.

My mind is racing, but some calm part of me points out that Cap's room is on this side of the tavern. I glance up at the wooden shutters that sit across the windows, then down at my discarded bow. Fuck. Might just work.

"Cover me," I toss over my shoulder at Jamil as I sling my sword into its sheath. The four brigands are closing now, but we're dead if we don't get help anyway.

"Cover you?!" He glances at me in disbelief, then sees what I'm doing.

I'm not the best shot with a bow, but near enough. I swallow, inhale, and release, and send two arrows—one after another—thunking into the wooden shutters that cover the windows. A sudden pit opens in my gut at the thought I might be shooting at an empty room, but a moment later, the shutters open.

Cap disappears immediately, and in the distance, I can just make out him bellowing down the hallways inside. Then I turn to look at our enemies, and I swallow.

Jamil might've drunk tonight, but it can't have been much as his movements are smooth and graceful. He spins, the two blades tracing uneven blazes of firelight into the air. Two have gone for him, and he's managing them, but the other two are grinning as they close on me.

One holds an enormous hammer, and the other a sword so blunt it must rely mostly on force to cut skin. I yank my own blade out and skip away from the fire just a little. Someone stepping in coals would be an excellent outcome of all of this, so I give myself the space.

I slash hard, warning them both back as they muscle toward me. I skip away from the hammer's heavy fall and dodge the sword-cut from the other, then spin, the movement certain and finally feeling right. I carve upward from below and into the swordsman's armpit. He roars in pain and dances back into the edge of the fire, then sideways. I draw my blade back and stab forward, through his heart, then bound toward the dying man to avoid another drop of the hammer.

There's a whistling sound, and the man closest to the tavern—the hammer-wielder—sprouts a bloody silver star out of his ear. He croaks, eyes widening and then fading, weaves, and falls to the ground.

I glance up. Rizzen is at the cap's window, and he nods in acknowledgment at my look, then sends another blade toward the opponents facing Jamil. I step in to make the most of the man's distraction and carve hard into his upper arm.

Rizzen's weapon thunks into his shoulder at the same moment, and I reverse my swing to slice into his thigh. He makes a gurgling sound of pain and topples sideways on top of his dead compatriot.

Grinning now, the rhythm of the fight settling in, I spin to lunge to Jamil's aid and carve through the back of the leather jerkin of the nearest enemy. He turns clumsily with a sound of pain and anger, and I regret not choosing the smaller brigand. This one is built like a bull, and the double-headed axe he holds makes me gulp.

Another shimmering weapon comes sailing through the air, and as he glances sideways toward it, I lunge, thrusting my sword point through his neck. Blood trickles down to my hand, and I shove deeper. Rizzen's blade falls short this time, into the coals of the fire, but the distraction was enough. The bull-shouldered man clutches at his throat and falls backward.

Twelve people appear around the side of the tavern building, all carrying torches and weapons. They bellow, and there's movement in the shadowy bush as the remaining brigands split.

I lean on my knees as Bols, Pulldark, and Cap join us by the fireside, Issian, Wens, and Morwell behind them, and the tavern-owner, hostlers, and barkeep pulling up the rear. "Thanks," I huff breathlessly. "And thanks to Rizzen. He saved us with those flashy blades."

"Handy in a pinch," Cap nods. His breath is like a brewery, and I wrinkle my nose before I realize what I'm doing. "How many did you two kill?"

"These you see here—seven—and one more off in the bushes shot by Des," Jamil replies. "Might have done a runner, though."

Bols, also in a miasma of alcohol, wanders in the direction he points, axe in hand. Is he still staggering? How much did he drink tonight? Pulldark heads in the opposite direction, Wens and Issian with him, to beat the bushes on the other side. I don't need to smell the old man to know he's probably just as pungent as the others.

"Good work, Jamil, Des." Cap nods to each of us. "And good thinking on getting us roused, Des. We'd have heard you eventually, though."

"We'd have been dead eventually," I say, smiling to take the sting out. How can he doubt that, with seven brigands dead at our feet? "But I'm sorry about your window."

"Gave me a start," Cap acknowledges, "but Rizzen was just across the hall, so he was in there quick."

"Turned the tide," Jamil agrees.

I feel a sudden chill. Rizzen had been at their side through all the drinking tonight. I have a vision of the star lodging in the brigand's head. Those blades could've hit us. I swallow my gorge.

Cap wanders off to send the tavern folk back to their beds. I sigh and glance up. Framed in the dim light of Cap's window stands Karina, gazing down. I smile wearily and raise a hand. She does the same. "Does this count as finishing our watch?" I ask Jamil.

A smile ghosts across his face. "Sounds fair to me."

I lift my sword, marveling at how heavy it feels, and balance it on my shoulder. It's bloody, and it'll get all over my clothes, but I'm already soaked in red. There's something extraordinary about the weariness that comes after a fight. I slip away back into the tav and labor up the stairs to my room.

The water in the jug beside the basin is cold, but I pour it out. I unbutton my shirt, fingers sticky with congealed blood, and go to peel it off my shoulders. There's a knock at the door. Probably Cap come to tell me I have to get down there and finish my shift. I sigh, too weary to be careful about being decent, and cross to open it.

It's Karina, wide-eyed and still tousled from bed, wearing a dressing gown tied firmly around her waist. I smile weakly, clutching my shirt closed. "Evening," I say. "Sorry about the look."

Karina swallows. "Are you hurt?" she says, her voice a little higher than usual. I shake my head. "No. Rizzen's blades kept me safe. Well, mine too."

"Thank the heavens," Karina murmurs. "That's a lot of blood."

"Not mine," I reply with a small smile. "Jamil and I are fine. They weren't the strongest fighters I've ever gone up against. Probably more desperate. They were aiming for stealth."

She bites her lip, still staring at me. After a moment, it feels awkward, and I add, "I really am alright, though, Karina. You don't have to worry. Just tired. But that's coz it's late." She jerks away, half as if she's shaking herself awake, but I realize it might sound like a hint for her to leave. "I didn't mean..."

A glimmer of her usual self-assurance reappears as she steps back from the door. "It's fine, Des. You need sleep, and we need you able to function tomorrow. I just wanted to make sure you were whole."

"Whole and entire," I reply, holding out my hands as if in proof. My shirt falls open a little more. Karina makes a sound somewhere between a whistle and an "oof," and turns away again as I turn red and clutch the two pieces of fabric back together in a fist. "Thanks for checking, though."

"Night," Karina throws over her shoulder as she walks away. I lean against the doorframe for a moment, letting myself watch her hips shift under her gown, then turn back to continue cleaning myself off.

# CHAPTER SIX

T he sunset is red-gold and blinding as we drive toward it, and though the light will linger long after the sun is down, Karina calls a halt early. She sends me a grin as we scatter to our respective tasks. 'Tis the tenth day on the road, and the setting up of camp is almost smooth now. I set myself to helping Issian brush the horses, then trail behind Besta to collect wood from the thick scrub around us.

We return to find the wagons and caravans encircling the fireplace, where Pulldark is readying a meal, looking grumpy it's his turn. "Ugh, not him again," Besta says as we draw closer. "He can't cook."

I suppress the smirk. He's right, unfortunately. "Lucky we still have some of that bread from Enishae, then, hmm?"

"And butter?"

I narrow my eyes. "Maybe. But at least olive oil."

"I like olive oil even better than butter," Besta says. "Mama says the more rare a thing is, the more precious it is, and I know cows are more rare than olive groves here, but..." He shrugs. "I like the taste better."

I grin. "The good news about that, Besta, is you'll never have to be wealthy to like what you put on your bread."

Besta cocks his head at me, then beams widely as he works out what I mean. Then he's off to find his mother, at the same speed he seems to do everything.

"Des? A hand?"

I glance off into the trees, where Cap rolls a broad log toward the camp. It's an impressive width and will seat several of us comfortably. I'm relieved I won't wind up having to volunteer to sit on the ground again.

Pushing the log with him, I seize the moment. "We're heading into bandit country," I say, quiet enough to keep it from the rest of the group. "Want me to do a scout before the sun's gone altogether? If there's the chance of a raid tonight, we'd best be prepared."

Cap sends me a dark look and doesn't reply.

I frown, and together we lever the log upright so we can fit it between the wagons. "Cap? I know this place. Camped here before. I can do a quick scan. You won't even miss me."

"Do you think I don't know my job, girl?" he hisses. "I am in charge, right? I know this road. Backward. I know where the bandits are, and this ain't it. Let me do my job."

I work my mouth for a second in shock at his tone. "I don't want to overstep," I begin, but falter when I see his gimlet eyes on me.

"Then don't." He pushes at the log, which falls with a giant thump into the middle of the camp, startling our chef and the cluster of others around the fire.

He stalks off, and I frown after him. I know this stretch of bush. It needs a scout. Why doesn't he trust me?

After we've eaten, Cap sends Jamil off to scout. It's dark by this time, and our chances of spotting anything have reduced significantly. I sigh. I put him in charge. Now I've got to stick by it.

Karina disappears to put Besta to sleep in the caravan they share. I sit and sip at the tea Issian brewed for us—lots of sweet, rich flavors, intended as an antidote to Pulldark's uninspiring fare.

Wens sits beside me with a groan. We both missed out on the log after all, but the blanket isn't so bad. "Karina asked me to tell you she needs to speak with you alone," Wens says in a low voice. "She'll be in my van."

I raise my brows. "She did? When?"

"Before she put Besta to bed."

I frown, but the look he gives me is both weighty with significance and a warning not to ask further questions. Great. This doesn't seem like a fun hookup; it seems more like sitting down with the boss to hear her concerns when I can do naught about them.

But there's not much to do but front up. So I rise, nod to everyone like I always do when I'm heading to relieve myself, and make my way around the back of the vans to Wens's. I wait until Bols has said something outrageous and everyone is reacting to him to tap gently on the door before I open it.

Karina is perched on the edge of the table centered in the room, her arms crossed, looking at me sideways. Not on the bed. If I needed confirmation of her intention, that's it. My belly sinks through my heels, and I gather myself to be properly professional. Ignore her curves. Ignore the way her coiled hair shifts around her head, keeping her face always partially in shadow. Ignore the uncurling deep in my gut. Deep breath.

"Wens said you wanted to see me?" I say in opening.

Karina gives me a wry smile, shifting so her bronze face is lit for a moment by the lantern hanging over the table and then falls back into shadow. "I feel I've been spending a disproportionate amount of my time trying to make clear to you I want more than that," she says, and the bluntness of the words makes my breath catch. "But," she adds, "it *is* business I need to talk to you about now." I blink at her, spinning like a top internally.

She watches me intently, then grins a little. "Oh, don't tempt me," she says, after a long moment of me struggling to work out what to say. "You give me that bemused look and all I want to do is be extremely clear."

My heart beats in my ears, and finally, I toss fate to the winds. It is what it is, even with all the complexity of her paying my wage.

I smile and have the satisfaction of seeing her gaze darken. "It's clear," I say, "but I'm not sure Wens would be alright with giving up his van for you to talk to me about work only to find us in his bed when he comes to sleep. Plus, it won't do good things for me with the captain if they hear us." I let my own gaze deepen on hers. "And they *would* hear us." She chuckles breathlessly in response, and it's all I can do to not cross the room and press my mouth against hers.

"So, I'll make you a deal. If you can restrain yourself until tomorrow night—that's when we're in Tibalt, no?—then I'll make sure we have some space and some actual privacy. A bed, even."

My breath hitches again, and proper desire cascades through me. I have to close my eyes a moment against it and wrench myself back together.

"But tonight," I add softly, "you have something you need to talk to me about, and that's what we're going to do."

I only find I've been slowly making my way across the tiny space toward her when the proximity is a little too much. Her face is right there, her lips slightly apart, her dark eyes pinned to my face, and I force a slow inhalation. I lick my lips, bite them, and then shove myself away and into the seat beside the table.

"I..." Her voice trails off, and she clears her throat. "You're right. Thank you." She doesn't sound entirely grateful, but I can't blame her. I'm both impressed and disappointed in myself for my own self-control.

She eases herself into the seat opposite and steeples her fingers together. "So. I need you to take over leading these mercenaries," she says, and her bluntness makes me almost dizzy. My lips part as if I'm going to speak, but I can't tell if I have nothing or too much to say. She raises a finger. "No, let me explain. I heard you with Cap this evening. You told him he should be scouting, and he ignored you. He sent Jamil out, but that was after the sun was already down." She shook her head. "You know what you're doing, and instead of respecting that, he's behaving like he's in a power struggle with you."

I fold my lips, thinking. "Yes, but this is the thing. I tried not to make it a power struggle. I've tried not to challenge him. At all."

She shakes her head. "I saw it, Des. You're not challenging him. I can't afford to have my caravan's safety compromised because the leader of my protection isn't prepared to take advice from a woman."

She says it so bluntly I blink. She's so sure it's because I'm a woman. I wish I could be as certain, but I've been doing this merc thing a bare handful of years, and Cap has been at it since I was still a suckling babe.

I sigh and press my fingertips into my forehead. "I don't think the others will follow me. That's the issue. If I did, I'd tell you to ditch Cap and let me take over." I think of Bols. "But they won't, not in a hundred years."

She meets my gaze, holds it. "You are better situated to assess that," she says after a long moment, sounding less than convinced, "but I can think of no other solution. We can't afford to turn back."

I jerk my head, then shake it more definitively. "No, I know. Besides, we're ten days in. Tyrasene is only another fortnight, maybe two tendays away. We're more than a third done. We can't turn back now."

She nods and tugs at her earlobe. "So... thoughts?"

My mouth quirks. "Many. Not many that are useful, but... Cap is good at what he does. He can wrangle the others, and that is valuable. I need to find a way to get on his good side." I smile. "Let me see if I can, and there's a chance there'll be someone else I know in Tibalt. Another sellsword who might be willing to take his place."

She cocks her head at me. "Alright, if that's how you want to play it. But, Des, I think you could do this. Are you really sure they're not just... questioning your competence because you're a woman? Coz I've seen it before, and that's *all* about them. It's got naught to do with what you can actually do."

I purse my lips regretfully. Half of me wishes I could tell if she was right. Maybe it'd be simpler if I knew I could trust my own skills. If I was sure I knew enough to lead. But I've only ever managed it with Petrus beside me.

Besides, even if she is right, it doesn't change how they see me, and that's the kicker. I raise my hands helplessly. "I wish they'd follow me, Karina, I really do, but I can't see it happening."

She sighs. "Alright. It's not a solution, not yet. But I'll give you a bit of time."

I nod slowly, then watch as her hand slides across the table to capture mine. I knew it was coming, but still, her fingers against my palm make my heart skip over. "I..." I stop, unable to remember what I had been going to say.

"Ugh, Des, this is *painful*." She laughs. "I don't think I've ever been this patient before."

I grin back, then capture her hand and stand up in the tiny space. I ease around until I'm above her, my knees nearly touching hers, our fingers laced together. Her head tilts back to look up at me, the long column of her neck presenting all those kissable places. My breath comes a little short, and the next thing I know, I've cupped the back of her head and drawn her up to me. I pause a long moment, her lips barely a hair's breadth from my own, her breath tickling my mouth, drawing out the agonizing pleasure of the *almost*.

And then I sigh, giving way just that little bit, and cover her mouth with my own. There's a moment of the sweetest yielding, and then Karina's mouth presses against me, her tongue tangling with mine.

I can't keep back the moan as desire surges through my body in response, and my hand slides from neck to shoulder to the dip of her waist and I'm pulling her against my body. She's all warm curves, the softness of her a contrast with the hunger of her mouth.

Her hands slide from my shoulders to grip a handful of my hair, and I gasp a little as she tugs my mouth away from hers. The denial only makes the desire clearer. My breath trembles.

She inhales swiftly through her open mouth, her eyelids flickering. "You..." she says, the words thick, barely formed. "You are just as dangerous as I thought you were." She chuckles low in her throat, then clears it.

The effort it takes to pull herself together is perversely satisfying. "If I don't stop now, I won't be able to," she whispers, releasing the fistful of my hair, "and Wens will not be pleased to find me unclothed in his van."

I smirk a little, swallow hard, then take a single step back and release my hold of her. "You're the boss," I murmur when I can manage words.

Karina's laugh is breathy, her voice almost back to its usual firm good humor. "Gods, don't tell me that. All I want is to rearrange this entire caravan's schedule so we can fuck all day, but I have"—she rolls her eyes—"responsibilities."

I take another step back, and she lunges forward to catch my hand. Once she has it, she slowly turns it over and peeks out from under her lashes at me as she trails her fingertips against my bared wrist. Every caress feels like ice and fire, desire following in their wake.

Then she raises my hand ever so slowly—so slowly the anticipation has my heart pounding—and presses soft lips to the center of my palm. The touch echoes between my legs, and I'm blinking with the effort of trying to keep from crossing the space between us. All I want to do is lose myself in her mouth again.

After we've spent a good minute staring into each other's eyes, I jerk my body away, make myself move. "Good night," I say, ridiculously disappointed despite the promise of what's to come. I turn away.

"You too, Des. I know I won't be settling straight to sleep."

I spin back to face her, aghast.

"Blessed heavens, woman, you can't be that cruel," I say, scandalized. "How am I meant to get a wink imagining that!"

She laughs, her head thrown back, and I shake mine in half mock-chagrin before easing out into the chill darkness outside.

Rizzen is passing, likely on his way back from taking a piss, and he jerks his chin at me in greeting. I return it, smiling despite a little curl of dread in my gut. If Cap's already annoyed I'm in the picture, it won't get better if he knows what's unfolding with Karina. But somehow, I can't keep hold of the caution, too distracted by the thought of Karina's bed and all I plan to do to her in it.

# CHAPTER SEVEN

I t's a tough trek getting to sleep that night. It's not only the promise of Karina, though that would be enough. I've already let my mind and my fingers wander tonight, and as lovely as that was, the afterglow has not proven enough to let me sleep.

It's also the problem of the captain, and of Karina's distrust of him. I wish I felt anywhere near as certain as she was that it was about my sex and not about my skills. She's not wrong about him not being cautious enough—he's so confident he already knows where the problems are. He was right to set the guard at Enishae, but not scouting?

I sigh. I haven't the first clue what to do about it. I think of the men, think of how different they are to the mercenaries Petrus and I used to select to travel along with us. It had made sense when Cap wanted to choose his own crew, but now it seems foolish to have shaken hands over that. Had Pink been able to join us... or any of the others, really...

I roll onto my side, snugging my blankets tighter around my shoulders. What can I possibly do to change either Cap or his view of me? Either would work.

Changing Cap is probably an impossibility. I've already tried getting him to drink less, and that's counted for shit.

Changing his view of me... I sigh aloud in my little tent. Changing his view of me is likely to require a whole bunch of drinking, of pretending. Play at being one of them. It sounds exhausting. But it's more or less what I've already been trying. Plus, that would likely mean spending my downtime with them, convincing them I'm on their side, and Karina's promise of the next town is not something I'm prepared to give up just so Cap might think I won't call him out for his lackadaisical approach to the safety of the caravan.

I roll onto the other side, hooking an elbow out over the blanket. There's only one other option. I keep compensating for his lazy ass. I close my eyes. It's the best compromise I can come up with. He'll still be here if things get hairy, and we need him to yank the other mercenaries into order. It'd be lives on the line if they chose that moment to not listen—chain of command and all that.

And, in the meantime, I do what I would do were I in charge, as much as I can, without his notice. He's going to hate it whenever he spots what's going on, so I'll have to be careful, but it's the best I can think of.

I let my mind wander back to Karina and her kiss, and it's in the promise of her that sleep claims me.

I wake early the next morning, well before the sun, and groan aloud. It's not just that I've promised myself I'll get up and scout before anyone else is awake and that moment is now and it's cold. It's also that I've woken knowing I've dreamed of her again. Of Liv. It's the same sick feeling in my gut, that awful blend of love and desire and fury and betrayal. The poison no antidote—no matter where I source the partners or how much time I let pass—can seem to counter.

Ugh. I shove the thoughts from my mind, determined not to let Liv poison anything else. Liv is the past, and right now, my priority is Karina—Karina and the caravan. Yanking on trousers and a shirt, I shove my feet into boots and am up, out, and into the morning before the chill air convinces me otherwise. We're heading into more dangerous terrain today, out of the bare flatlands that surround the Red Desert and into bushier, hillier landscape.

As if to mark it, Liza and I disturb a cluster of kangaroos as I follow the ever-widening spiral I use to scout with. When the kangaroos are resting, you know the land is greener.

I find nothing. It's far from the distance we'll travel as a caravan, but it does mean the morning should be safe. Yawning, I urge Liza back to camp. I give her a quick brush and a pat before I wander off for a morning piss, grateful I'm not seen by any of the mercs. No doubt Cap would rib me silly. Maybe it is that I don't know what I'm doing, but I'd rather do this extra bit of work to make sure we're all safe.

"Where'd you go?" Besta asks, bouncing around me as I make my way to the fire, where Issian has taken responsibility for the morning's congee. "Did you take Liza out?"

I grin and tweak his nose. "She likes a good run occasionally," I say, "and she doesn't get it wandering alongside the caravan."

He nods almost as fast as he's bouncing. "Can you show me the juggle thing again? I nearly had it last time!"

"Hmmm," I say dubiously. "How's about an exchange? I need some breakfast."

He looks almost delighted to have a challenge. "I'll get your congee just how you like it!" I can't help but smile as he bounds off ahead of me.

# CHAPTER EIGHT

We make the tavern early. It's early afternoon, really, only an hour or so after lunch.

"I'll take the back," I call to Cap, who nods. It's important to have a rider for the back half of the caravan coming into towns like these. Sometimes the locals are light-fingered, and if there's a branch of the Rogue—an organized crime ring that operates across Rescalin—it can mean losing more than a few baubles.

I urge Liza forward and scoop around the last wagon in the caravan—the vulnerable tail. Rizzen throws me a sardonic salute from his place perched on its back. He's enough of a deterrent.

I set myself to weave between the wagons, dipping my head at each of the crew, protection and caravan drivers both, but it's uneventful. I almost wish someone would try something. It'd stop me worrying I'm missing the obvious signs of criminal activity, and worrying that, because I alone have missed them, none of us will be ready to react until it's too late. Gods, distrusting your leader is unpleasant.

It doesn't take long, though, and the wagons and vans are carefully locked up, the tavern's hostlers helping with backing the vehicles into a lockable, guarded warehouse, and with the feeding, watering, and brushing of the horses. I save Liza until last, using long strokes to clear her coat of the dust of the road. She revels in the attention.

"You like this life!" I say to her, almost accusingly. "Even without Petrus and Ebony?" She gives me what passes for a horsey grin, and I rub her nose, appreciating the warm velvet of it. "Yeah, I like this caravan too," I confide, "and it's making me think..."

It's too early—much too early by half—to wonder about these things out loud, but it's almost scary how swiftly my mind skitters forward. It's the warmth of it; it fills me.

It's not just Karina, though I am enjoying the promise of that, but it's also Besta, and Wens and Issian and Morwell—the family, the closeness. It's a little like the troupe in some ways, I think as I stroke across Liza's ribs, but the troupe was so full of power play and catfighting and one-upmanship that it was difficult to feel ever fully at ease. And that was before Liv's hot-and-cold, cruel-and-generous, fickle-and-steadfast nature made the troupe agony to be in.

No, it's not like that. This is actual family. Almost like it was with Petrus, before he blindsided me with his declaration. I blink the dust from my eyes. Warmth and acceptance and ease. I can't deny the longing.

"But it's mostly Karina. How could I have missed it, all those times traveling with them and Petrus?" I sigh, shaking my head. "No bigger regret than missing out on good sex, right?"

Liza hurrumphs as if I'm being ridiculous, which, of course, I am. The Petrus in my head snorts at me. It had been something Petrus was very clear on. "If there's a possibility, and the one you want doesn't want you, there's no harm in showing yourself others do." My gut sinks a little as I realize he had probably been talking about us that whole time.

"What's taking you so long, woman?" Karina's voice, dark like whiskey, echoes in the dimly lit stable.

I startle, nearly dropping the curry comb. "I—" My heartbeat picks up, and a strange nervousness unfurls in my gut. Nervousness? Gods, that's all I need.

"I booked the fanciest room they have," she continues.

Her footsteps are slow, uncertain almost, and I wonder for a moment, as I hook the curry comb on the nail by the stall gate, whether she might be as unsettled as me.

We almost surprise each other as we appear around the corner of the stall. For a long moment, I gaze at her. She grins back at me, that same knowing grin from the morning we set off, the one that had me disoriented. But this time, I know the path before us, so I grin back, and it's all too satisfying to watch a slow flush crawl up her cheeks.

After swiftly scanning the stable, I step toward her. I grasp her wrist firmly and spin her like we're dancing but end with her back pressed against the stall gate. It shifts, clunks, as she gasps in a little breath. I press against her, the length of my body pinning her to the rough wood, her arm above her head, and watch as her eyes darken and her lips part. "Gods, is that a promise?" she asks as I slide my hand from her wrist down. "Tell me it's a promise."

I laugh. Moving slowly enough it's a sweet agony for me, drawing out the anticipation for us both, I tilt my head and run my lips gently down the column of her neck, down to the curve where it meets her shoulder, bared by her chemise.

My fingers slip to the top button, loosening the neck just a little further. I pause for a moment here and let my breath cascade across her skin. When she finally shivers, I bite, my teeth grazing hard against her flesh. She moans in my ear, and the sound resonates into my sex, desire flooding me.

I'm panting when I pull back, just a little. "Did you mention a bath?" I say, and even I'm impressed by the husky drawl in my voice. Karina's eyes flutter open, and the sight makes me draw a slow breath. "Never mind." I wrap my arms around the length of her and cover her mouth with mine, sinking into her warmth. She's all softness and hunger, her hands knotting in my cropped hair, then drawing down the back of my neck. It sets all the fine nerves there alight.

There's a sound from outside, which I dismiss at once as irrelevant, but my mind prods me back, and I gasp, breathless, as I struggle to pull away. I force myself to step back, almost jerking away, and turn to face whoever's footstep that is jangling toward the stable. I take another step, setting myself between

Karina and the door, giving her a chance to straighten her clothes and pull herself upright.

"Oh, it's you. I thought everyone was already done. Sorry." Issian peers beyond me at Karina, and I see the light dawn in his eyes. "Oh, I'm sorry, I shouldn't—I mean—let me just..." The man dithers on the spot, taking a series of steps in three directions as his face turns to beet, and then, with an awkward tug at his hat, he's gone.

I turn back to Karina, laughter burbling up inside me. She's already bent double, struggling to breathe enough to laugh aloud. She hasn't even tugged her chemise back into alignment or done the button up. Catching her hands to keep her upright, I chuckle, trying to keep it quiet enough Issian won't feel too terribly mocked. "The poor man," Karina says when she can finally manage words. "He's known I wanted you for, oh, a good year or so, but he always turns that shade when I mention it. And now..."

"It's a risky business, entering a stable unannounced," I say, still giggling, "but it's probably a good idea to take this somewhere..." I've worked out my own ways of staying safe while pursuing my desires over the years, but I can't ever quite forget being kicked out of home, and out of my village, when Liv took me to her bed.

"...more comfortable?" she says wickedly, and I grin.

"Oh, if we must," I say. "You did seem to quite like the post, though."

Her breath catches a little in her throat. "Well, when we get to telling each other what we like, you'll understand why, I suspect."

Fucking blessed heavens. My lips part, and I can't work out what to say to that for a long moment, until she giggles. "It's alright, I can go first," she says archly. She sweeps past me, her skirts brushing against my legs, and I feel like I might lose my balance.

As she steps out of the stable, I'm only a step or two behind her. I catch sight of the captain leaning against the post of the tavern porch, gazing out across the courtyard. His gimlet eyes are fixed on us, and he already has a tankard in hand.

"I'll be right in," I call after her. "Thanks for checking in about the horses." It's a poor cover, but I can't quite rally the concern over what Cap might wonder about the two of us. We're both in Karina's employ, and frankly, my main worry is that he's not doing his job.

As I cross the sandy yard to greet him, Bols and Pulldark exit the tavern, tankards in hand. "'Bout bloody time we had a decent drink," Bols announces. He drinks long and deep, then belches. I catch the scent of it as I step up onto the porch and can't quite guard my reaction. Bols looks satisfied.

"You joinin' us, lass?" Cap asks. "You been working hard if you just finished up with the horses." His gaze is unwavering, and I draw myself up for the play. He's like the audience member we saw once in Umalet when I was doing my first juggle before Liv came on stage. He'd carried rotten tomatoes into the crowd and then watched closely for any tiny flaw, any excuse to toss the stinking fruit.

"Liza deserved a good rubdown," I say, and I pull a grin onto my face. "She's worked harder than I have, I reckon."

"True dat," Pulldark says, and there's a note of darkness in his tone.

I want to roll my eyes, but I resist. "You can have what's left of mine, if you want," Bols slurs, thrusting his tankard toward me. It's not intended as generosity. The gleam in his eyes is all about seeking my reaction.

I chuckle. "You're giving away beer now, Bols? That's not like you. I mean, if you're sure the barkeep didn't piss in it, I'll take whatever's on offer!"

His round, red face gets gleeful, so I gather myself, reach out, and drink the whole half-pint down without stopping for breath. It's enough to shift the mild air of hostility. I grin broadly at them. "Err... scull? Thanks, Bols. Might go grab myself a top-up."

It's agony, walking into the tavern and ignoring the stairwell I know leads up to the rooms, where Karina is waiting for me to climb the stairs and take her, but I make myself move straight to the bar and order two tankards. The barkeep is busy, so I get some space to work out what I'll do next.

These men... They'll claim they want me to stay and drink with them. It'll be a lie, of course—none of them want a killjoy sitting by them. They're going to want me gone, but they'll want to complain to each other about me when I go.

"You can manage one drink, Des," I tell myself. I heft the tankards, nodding thanks to the bartender. "One drink, then leave them be." There's a voice in my head reminding me I'm meant to be keeping them from the worst excesses of drink, given we're on the road early tomorrow and headed into prime brigand territory. Without confirming me as a killjoy who won't have their back? Impossible.

I blow out a breath. This trying-not-to-be-the-leader thing is harder than just being declared boss. Maybe I should've taken Karina up on her suggestion.

Jamil and Rizzen have joined the others on the porch, and Bols has dragged a second bench over. They're all sitting and guffawing about something. I thrust the tankard into Bols's hands. "Here."

"Aww, Des, you shouldn't have!" The insincerity in his voice makes the others laugh.

"Oh, if you don't want it, then," I say playfully, and reach to take it back.

"Never said that," he protests, and the others laugh even harder. Success. Now... One drink. I can handle one drink.

# CHAPTER NINE

**M**y head is buzzing a little by the time I tread the stairs up to Karina's room. I drank my beer probably a little too fast. The promise I'd made myself—that at the bottom of the tankard, I'd have done my duty to make these men trust that I'm like them—may not have been the smartest move.

As I climb, I think of how Karina's mouth fell open when I slammed her body against the post in the stable. Her chemise sliding away from that heavenly brown skin. The tip of her tongue touching the back of her teeth as she grinned at me. By the time I raise my knuckles to her door, desire coils heavy in my gut.

"Come in," she says, her voice low and calm.

Almost smiling at the effect just that has on me, I turn the doorknob.

She's still dressed, reclining against pillows on the bed. Her skirts are caught up around her legs, revealing acres of bronze thigh, and her chemise is still slipped sideways, her shoulder exposed. It makes me swallow, remembering that tiny button between my fingers earlier.

Finally, my gaze reaches hers. She looks unimpressed, her brows raised as if expecting an explanation.

"Apologies for running late, ma'am," I murmur, stepping into the role in response. I glance at the ground and then back up at her as if ashamed. "I was detained."

For a moment, she just looks at me, her mouth pursed, as if trying to decide how annoyed she is. Wickedness curves her lips. "Apologize properly, girl," she snaps. "On your knees."

She swings her legs out of bed to stand. I grin, hastening toward her and skidding down onto my knees, my hands pressed together below my chin in a gesture that begs forgiveness. It's an old and sacred custom from Sconda; I remember Picton teaching us.

"I am so very sorry, ma'am," I say breathily, and then reach out, only half pretending the quivering of my fingertips as they slide under her skirts and slowly, slowly up.

"You are *not* forgiven," she replies after a long moment, just as I reach her knees. Her voice is a little strangled, and I glance up to see her mouth gone soft with desire.

I smile to myself. "Will you let me prove how very sorry I am?" I whisper. My hands close on the warmth of her thighs, and desire unfurls in my gut.

"I feel like I should punish you first." Her voice is so thick I can barely make the words out.

"You can punish me later, ma'am," I say. The skin of her inner thighs under my rough thumbs is like satin and velvet together. "I promise."

"Well, you do sound sorry."

Permission granted, I push gently back, then rise and follow her, my mouth capturing hers. She moans against my lips, and it thrums through me, tangling the warmth in my sex and making it flare. My hands still linger on her thighs, and I draw them a little higher, high enough to discover she's not wearing any underwear.

She planned for me coming upstairs.

The knowledge makes my blood soar, and I'm nibbling down her throat, my fingers against those tiny buttons again. Her chemise falls back, revealing a band of soft dark skin that draws a line down her soft torso to her skirts. My breath is short.

"You're so beautiful," I whisper, kissing down the line until I reach her belly. She arches her back, reaching behind her to unbutton her skirt.

I feel the waistband loosen and snug my fingers into it to tug it just a little lower, the anticipation like a string thrumming between us. I kiss across her belly until I find the point where her skin dips, where the bone of her pelvis surfaces. Opening my mouth against her flesh, I gnaw gently until she moans helplessly, as if my tongue were somewhere else.

I smile and kiss across to the other side. We both shiver as I cross the line of dark curls peeping above the waistband. My teeth graze across the bone, over and over, and she gasps, already moving against me.

I raise my head but don't hold back my grin. "May I?"

For a moment, she can't even register that I've said anything, and then it turns to frustrated amusement. "Have I been unclear in some way?" She knows I'm teasing, and I know she's pretending frustration. Well, half pretending.

I grin as I tug her skirt away and onto the floor, then gaze for a moment at the gorgeous fullness of her. The soft roundness of her belly, the strength and curve of her thighs, and between them all, the triangle of dark curls.

She raises her head to see what precisely I'm about, and I grin at her. "You're stunning."

"And *you're* lovely, but would you mind hurrying it along? I've waited long enough for this."

I laugh. "What is it you're wanting? ... This?" I kiss the top right corner of the triangle. "Or... this...?" I kiss the top left, but this time, I'm running teeth over her skin, and she shivers and gasps. "Or... is it somewhere..."

I trail my tongue from the point of her hip, a long line running down to her inner thigh. Her leg turns out, revealing the dark pink of her quim, already slick and silver in the low light. She makes a choked noise of pleasure, frustration, and amusement.

"Somewhere there," she says, her voice caught between grouchy and entertained.

"Hmm, I wouldn't want to get it wrong," I tease.

"Oh, I think there's little risk of that," she murmurs back, "but I can help you figure it out if you like..."

Her hands slide into my hair, and I grin. "Well, if you think I need the help..."

She laughs, a breathy sound lost in desire. "I think you know *exactly* what you're doing." Her fingers grip my hair in fists against my head, making my breath catch.

"Oh," I say finally, and she draws me closer to her. "I'm so sorry, I've been so confused. Is it *this* you're wanting?"

I descend abruptly, wrapping my mouth around her clit and setting my tongue to it with a will. She gasps first at the contact, then groans more loudly than she has so far as the pleasure chases the fulfillment of anticipation.

I mold my mouth to her, finding by instinct the rhythm that elicits the strongest reaction. My own desire is rising, filling me like warmth, my sex already clenching against itself, lubricous and fluid. It's barely a moment before she's crying out, those glorious thighs closing against my ears, muffling the gorgeous heady groans of her release.

It's just the beginning. I don't even pause, but gentle my touch a little until the sensitivity dissipates, catching the wave before the ebb and pushing it higher again.

This time, I slip a finger inside her, warm and saturated, followed by another as she arches her back. The tips of my finger press hard upward, harder than I'd dare on the delicate flesh my mouth continues to consume, pressing her higher, further and further.

Her thighs quiver, tension thrumming through her, then a great cascade of pleasure, and this time, I hear every sound.

She draws me up against her on the bed, still befuddled with afterglow as she tugs my shirt free, makes short work of my buttons, and sheds her own chemise, then we're pressed together and her hand slides between my legs.

It's then I discover her intended punishment. Over and over, she brings me to the brink of orgasm, first with her fingers, then with her mouth against my breast and her knee at my quim. Then, finally, the delicious torture of her lips against my clit and her fingers buried deep inside me is simply too much, and I clutch her head to me as I come against her mouth.

# CHAPTER TEN

I blink into wakefulness late the next morning, the light making bright bars around the edges of the curtain. Karina is nowhere to be seen, and though this makes my gut sink, I know she's likely breaking her fast with Besta.

I sigh, taking the space as a delightful moment to stretch against myself, feeling all the warm-and-achy aftermath of our lovemaking. I gaze about me. The bedclothes are crumpled into piles on the bed, even the sheets tugged away from the mattress, and I can spot various articles of my clothing strewn across the floor. I grin and stretch again, thinking of Karina. A *good* night.

I pad across the room to pour myself a glass of water from the elegant jug sitting on the table by the mirror. It's a beautifully appointed room—I'd barely noticed last night—with graciously carved wooden furniture and burgundy-and-blue rugs laid against the wooden floor. It's fancier than anywhere Petrus and I could have afforded to stay. I take a deep breath. I suppose it wouldn't be so hard to get used to this kind of thing.

The admission to myself sets my heart pounding for reasons I don't fully understand. I like Karina. A lot. It's not a big, dramatic love, like with Liv, but it feels like it could be more mature. We get along. She likes me. She has a family and a business I can understand my place in.

And it's a warm place. Issian, Wens, Morwell, even Shameela—they're all easy to be with. Besta, the hilarious and cute center of their little world. It would be so easy to let my world turn around him too. It's a calm space, one where the risk of life and limb is occasional rather than regular. Where I might not have to lean so hard into violence. A glare from behind a market stall. The revealing of an inch of blade when I needed to make a point.

It feels dangerous, to let myself want it. It had been what I thought I'd found when my mother kicked me out and the village followed suit, when I'd taken up with Picton's troupe, following Liv. I'd found Petrus and Picton and Umina and the others. And then Petrus and I had had to leave, Liv too poisonous a presence and too central to Picton's plans for us to stay. For a while, it had been me and him, and then, well... and then he'd walked out. And now this, offered openly, with no strings I can see, no poison at its heart.

I sigh and let it go. Borrowing trouble, I tell myself. Just let it be. It's weeks 'til we reach Tyrasene. More than enough time to see whether what's between Karina and I could carry all that.

It makes me want to go and find her, though, to read some measure of reassurance in her dark eyes. It's the work of a moment to dress myself, though I know I need to find my own room and my bag of clothes before I find Cap and the others. Reappearing in the same outfit I'd had on the day before would not be discreet, and we need not confirm the suspicions I read in Cap's gaze.

I eventually find my own room, and the bags I'd handed to the tavern's hostler-busboy-general help are stacked by the bed. I find myself a shirt and scrub at a stain on my pants—a gift from Karina, I realize—before I give up and root out a less-grubby pair from the bags.

I've probably missed the chance to get a proper launder of all my things, but I can't say it wasn't worth it. I run my thumb against my bottom lip, remembering gazing up at Karina, watching desire dawn in her eyes. I give myself a moment to let the resonance of the night shiver through me.

I toss water over my face, shove my hair back, and give myself a quick grin in the pockmarked mirror. Do I look recently fucked? Do I care? So what if they know.

I hasten downstairs and smile as I hear Besta's voice resounding from the big barroom downstairs. Issian's quiet remonstrance, Wens's bluff laughter. And there, a counterpoint: Karina's. It makes me smile broader and sigh.

"Sleep well, Des?" Bols's voice booms behind me. "You left in a hurry last night."

"Surprised to see you up and about, frankly, Bols," I say. "You looked set to drink the night away." I give him a sideways once-over. He's red-eyed, pale, and puffy, and even as I watch, he belches heavily and winces as he swallows down what might have been actual vomit. Ugh.

"Enjoyed meself last night," Bols says equably. "I know how to enjoy a good beer or two."

"Or three or four," I can't help but reply.

"Or five or six, but who's counting?" Bols says, as if we're conspirators. "So long as that harridan Karina don't know, what's the harm, I say?"

"Mmpf." I limit myself to the noncommittal sound, biting my tongue against the part of me that wants to defend Karina. They were off duty. Drinking while off duty is allowed.

I step forward into the room, and her dark eyes slide to mine as the knowing, helpless smile dawns on her face. I turn to give Bols the benefit of the full smile so he's distracted from seeing the two of us grinning like teenagers at each other. "Breakfast?"

It's early afternoon when we trundle away from Tibalt with me in the lead. The plan is to reach a campsite Cap remembers before sundown. It'll be tight, but we're carrying a pot full of stew from the tavern kitchen and enough big loaves to have us sorted for the next few days, so at least dinner will be easy.

Karina's in the driver's seat on the first wagon, and as we ride, she gives a low wolf whistle that makes me turn in my seat, half-indignant, half-amused, and mostly pleased. "I have a plan for tonight," she says softly. "I've arranged for Besta to sleep in Issian's van. There's a shelf you can put a mattress on, too small for an adult but it'll be fine for my boy."

I glance sideways. "You confirmed his suspicions?"

Karina sends me a smug little smile. "Well, I suppose so. He was way past suspecting, though. He's known me a goodly long time. Knows me. Knows what I like."

I echo her secret grin. "And what do you like?"

She tilts her head. "About *that* I think you likely know a damn sight more than Issian now."

I can't keep back the laugh, even though it feels like a giveaway—all depth and warmth. "Well, I am enjoying learning. And I do feel there's maybe a few more lessons on my list."

"Promises, promises," she says, her tone mock-severe but her grin wicked.

It trickles directly to my sex, and I laugh again, then clear my throat. "If I don't do a patrol run, I'm going to be climbing up there to find out what lessons exactly you could teach me from the driver's seat of that wagon," I say in a low voice. "And as glorious as that sounds, I don't think either of us wants to be announcing ourselves quite so loudly."

"Mmm... you're right. You do make a decent amount of noise," she muses.

I chuckle again. "Don't tempt me."

"I could think of a dozen things this driver's seat could be used for," she says.

I lick my lips. "Only a dozen?"

"'Til tonight, then?"

"I'll find my way to your van after I go to bed," I say back. "I won't keep you waiting."

"Be sure you don't."

I urge Liza into a quick spin to ride the length of the caravan, trying to focus on possible threats, not Karina's promise.

We ride into camp as the sun is disappearing, and I take responsibility for setting the fire and putting the stewpot on the tripod sitting over it. The loaves I place on the rocks set around the fireplace to let them warm. They smell divine.

Dinner is raucous and enjoyable, despite Cap and his men being taciturn with hangovers. Wens starts up a song as soon as he's done eating, and Besta's clear soprano dances over the top. I grin and turn a pot over to pound out a beat, while Morwell fetches his precious lap harp.

And then Karina scoops Besta up to settle him to sleep. Issian avoids my eyes as he follows them, much to my amusement. "I'll be turning in soon," I announce to all and sundry. I want to be clear.

"Not joining us for a drink, then?" Jamil hoists a bottle from behind the log he's sitting on. "You barely drank anything last night." My gut sinks. Drinking on duty? And that's the hard stuff too, in a bottle. How are we meant to keep a proper watch with this going on?

"Too busy judging us?" Bols says, eyes narrowing.

I laugh, aiming for nonchalance. "You make your choices, I make mine," I say lightly, my heart sinking.

Last thing any of them need is more drink. Hungover protection details count for shit. I wonder if Cap will say anything, but he grins at me as he pulls out another bottle to swig from, this one even bigger than Jamil's. I hold back a heavy sigh. I know I should stay and see if I can moderate their drinking, but that sounds unpleasant. And the thought of Karina—warm, sexy Karina—on her own in her caravan is too much to bear.

"C'mon, Des, just a quick drink," Cap says, his black eyes fixed on me.

"Oh, just one, then. You've twisted my arm," I say, giving way on this one in the hope they'll ease up when I disappear. I hear Petrus's scorn in my head that I'm crossing yet another line, but what am I meant to do?

Cap passes the bottle through Pulldark and Rizzen, each of whom take a long draw, and then to me. I brace myself, filling my mouth and swallowing hard to quash any gasp or cough—the things I know will count for weakness among this crew. "Mmm. A fine vintage," I say, playing at posh. "And is that an oaken barrel I taste?"

They all snicker and laugh, and for a moment, it's all ease. Success.

Out of the corner of my eye, I see Karina walk slowly up the steps to her caravan door. I've missed the glance over her shoulder, but her head is in profile, and she's hiked up her skirt to reveal the back of her thigh. She knows I'm watching her, and I grin to myself.

"Alright, one last drink and then I'm for bed," I say. "At least 'til it's my watch. C'mon, who's feeling generous?" I beckon each hand at the two bottles, my gut heavy with dread. They're on their way to empty.

# CHAPTER ELEVEN

I pause as I leave my tent the next morning, heading into the trees to piss. It's early, dark still. Cap had been noisy about not needing to scout last night, and no doubt that'd be his defense if Karina asked about the empty bottles. This bit of the road is safe, he says. I'm tempted to clamber back into my bedroll for a moment. Is it even worth scouting? If he says it's safe...

My gaze catches on Karina's van, and my breath hitches at the memory of Karina's hands knotting in the bedsheet as I wrapped my tongue around her clit. I lick my lips, tuning back in to the ache between my thighs marking a job well done. The woman can fuck.

I narrow my eyes, hesitating by my tent. The sun will be up soon. If we're sending a scout before we break camp, like Petrus and I always used to do, we've got little time for it. If I do it now and there's nothing, I don't even have to tell Cap I went. He won't have to be pissy about me challenging his authority, or whatever it is he thinks I'm doing when I do his job for him. And if I find something, well... that'll be a bridge to cross then.

I stiffen my jaw, and instead of returning to my bedroll, wander over to the line of horses. As I pass the ring of logs around the fire, I spot three bottles, all empty. Liza is napping at the end of the row, her saddle set on a blanket nearby. I heft it up, and she startles a little as I place it on her back. "Morning, girl," I say softly. "You and I are going to do a little exploring."

I do what I always do when scouting, riding in an ever-increasing spiral until I spot something interesting. And I do.

It's on the other side of the road from where we've set up our camp, amongst a set of low hills. The perfect spot for an ambush, by which I mean, it doesn't have a reputation yet, so it's where I'd set myself up were I trying to harry this stretch of road.

The hills are mostly green and grassy but interspersed with bushy thickets and enormous gray rocks. Lots of opportunities for concealment. Indeed, I don't even see the thready smoke until I'm gazing down into the valley where they've set up camp.

I edge my way amongst the scrub, finding the bush here thick with grasstrees, their fountaining blade-like green leaves good cover. Once I'm in, the leaf litter underfoot stops the hoofbeats of our passage from echoing. I urge Liza forward. I need to know numbers.

I pause for a long moment, gazing over the quiet camp. They're not awake yet, but I don't doubt they'll be waking soon, and I need to be far away by then. There's eight tents, and on first glance, this seems like a good thing for us. Eight brigands, and with our numbers, we'll win, even if the whole crew are hungover.

But as I stare across the clearing, I realize it's not so simple. Five tents are larger, probably fitting at least two, but maybe three souls in each. Suddenly, the numbers are not leaning our way. Thirteen we could maybe handle, though it wouldn't be fun, and we'd likely take some damage, which might force us back to Tibalt. Eighteen and we're likely in trouble. More than that...

I swallow a lump in my throat. We're likely in trouble.

I urge Liza gently through the brush until we're distant enough to ensure the campful of brigands won't hear us, then I tighten my thighs against her ribs. She doesn't need more urging, and I ride, already making plans.

We need Besta and Karina in the caravan in the center of the long train. Rizzen with his throwing knives on a rooftop is likely best—preferably the same van.

Jamil's broad shoulders and Bols's bulk near the front to warn them back, and covering Issian and Wens. Pulldark's bow at the back, up on a driver's seat. And Morwell, Cap, and me on horseback, ready to pull tight to protect the line.

My gut is all tension. Better still would be for the protection crew to ride ahead of the caravan, draw out the brigands or beard them in their den. I grit my teeth, remembering the promise I'd made so glibly to Shameela in Pastira.

I ride into camp, right up to the fireside. Cap, Pulldark, Bols, and Rizzen are clustered around its warmth, and they're all drunkard-pale and waxy. Fucking perfect.

Besta and Karina are just exiting their caravan. Her lips are still ruddy from being kissed so thoroughly last night, but I refuse to let myself be distracted. "There's brigands out there," I announce firmly. "We need to make a plan."

Cap rises to his feet, his face like a thundercloud about to spit lightning.

"Plan, schman," Bols says behind him. "Bit of a fight got you nervy, Des? Don't you worry your sweet little head. The big menfolk'll protect you."

"There's at least thirteen, probably many more," I say flatly. "We should be able to manage them, but we're going to need to think this through."

For a moment, Cap's gaze darkens further, and then, as if recalling his audience, he laughs. It sounds forced to my ears, but I've ridden with this man too many times. "Oh, Des, they're probably just Rovers! They like this part of the road. No one ever has a go here, and even if they did, like Bols said... we've been waiting for a bit of excitement."

I stare at him a moment. Knowing my gaze is chilly doesn't help me warm it up. I chew the inside of my cheek 'til I taste copper. Fuck him. Fucking careless fucking bastard.

Insisting won't get me anywhere, that much is clear. I glance across at Karina, her arm protectively across Besta's chest as he leans back unconsciously into her warmth, his wide eyes pinned to mine. He's scared.

Karina's chin juts forward, and I realize with horror I've walked straight into it. It's going to turn into what I never wanted it to be. A showdown, and right here, with eighteen fucking brigands ready to descend. We can't afford to be without protection with them this close.

And that means we have to keep this fucking crew, with their fucking captain, onside. It's like a game of Royals where I've backed myself into a corner. I cannot leave Besta and Karina with only my blade for protection. I'm decent with my sword, but I can't take on eighteen men and live.

"We'll ride on when we're packed up," Cap says, taking his coffee cup from Jamil and staying on his feet. "And you'll see, Des. There'll likely be nothing happen today, and even if there is, you needn't worry. *You'll* be safe. We're here."

My gut curdles with fury. He's impugning my courage, picking a fight. My first urge is to pull a weapon on him, but somehow, I resist. Karina can see my anger, I know, and I know, too, what she thinks the answer is. And that answer would likely see the captain take the other mercs and head back to Tibalt. We can't afford that. I lick my lips and nod once, then walk Liza back out of the circle of the wagons and caravans.

As I strike my tent, I pull from my bags the bandolier I hardly ever wear and sling it across my body, arranging it so it doesn't interfere with the draw of my sword. I'm not great at throwing daggers—haven't practiced nearly enough—but whatever additional weaponry I can carry, I'm going to.

Every dagger and blade I own gets tucked into crevices and corners until I'm fairly bristling. My mind races, trying desperately to find an out. Is it better to go back to Tibalt, to blow Karina's schedule? But that puts their business at risk—we'd definitely be late to Tyrasene if we turned tail. And we'd need to find a new crew, and there were no likely-looking mercs in Tibalt yesterday.

I close my eyes. What a fucking mess.

"You two stay out of sight in here," I tell Karina and Besta, opening the door to their caravan in the center of the line as we're readying to head out from camp. "It'll be the safest spot. Lock the door. I'm going to see if Rizzen will ride on the rooftop. It'll give his blades better range."

Karina grips my arm. "We have to do this, Des. Now is the moment. You don't have to do anything. I'll tell Cap he's been demoted and you're the new boss."

I shake my head. "We can't, Karina. We can't lose them, not now. We need every skerrick of muscle we can muster."

Her mouth falls open as she follows my logic, and fear shows in her eyes for the first time. I wonder again whether it would be best to turn around, head back. But that will take Karina and Shameela under, and I can't be responsible for that.

I shut the door on the two, grit my teeth, and go to find Rizzen. He meets my eyes and looks aside. "Cap's already spoken to me," he says, forestalling my words. "I'm not to do anything you tell me."

I tilt my head in exasperation and blow out a breath. "There are brigands out there, Rizzen."

Rizzen's expression is sympathetic, but he mounts his horse without another word.

I swallow hard and turn away to clamber up into my own steed's saddle. Liza's with me, at least. She can feel my jitters, her hoofs shifting uneasily. "Hush, lass," I say, patting her neck. "We'll need every last nerve for today's ride."

And then, without further preparation, we're riding out.

# CHAPTER TWELVE

"Ⓝo sign of nothing," Cap says around mid-morning, with triumphant satisfaction. "Guess you were mistaken, Des."

Bile burns in my gut. "We'll see, I suppose."

"Nothing to see," he spits, angry again, "because there's nothing there. I've done this road a dozen times. There's never any risk here. Just Rover camps scattered around. The real risk is the road down into Tyrasene itself."

I shake my head. "Well, that's definitely one risky patch, but I know what I saw, and this"—I nod my head forward—"is the perfect spot for an ambush."

We're about to travel into the deep valley between two hills, the green surface of them scattered with enormous gray rocks. The road is narrow enough between the two inclines it can easily be blocked. "Little wonder they'd pick this spot. No one knows it, so they're not wary. They can set a wagon across it and the caravan has to stop." Cap makes a dismissive noise, and I shake my head, adding, "Stick a few archers behind those rocks and they can pick us off easy." I'm almost wheedling, and I hate it.

"Don't get yourself nervy now, Des," Bols says behind me as we enter the beginning of the valley.

"Cap!" Karina's voice is already blazing, and I turn with pleading eyes. This is the last place we can afford this kind of confrontation. She's barreling down the length of the train, frowning. Anger is in every line of her body. "Cap, I need a word."

"Of course, ma'am," he says politely, dismounting to face her. I climb out of the saddle as well. "How can I help?"

Karina is significantly shorter than him, but she's full of righteous fury, hands pinned to her hips. If I wasn't feeling the prickling between my shoulder blades I always get when archers are around, I'd likely grin with desire. "If you can't listen to Des, I am going to have to ask you to step down. Now." Her tone is firm.

Cap's gaze is pure puzzlement. "Ma'am? I listen to Des, as I listen to all members of my crew," he says reasonably, "but I also know this road, and I know where the risks are. You've entrusted me with the caravan's safety, and I swear to you—"

"Mama!" Besta yells, cutting him off.

The boy races up the line of wagons and caravans, and we all turn to look at him. His face is a picture of horror. The next moment, a brigand steps out from between two wagons—where Bols was meant to be riding, I note absently—and catches him, one hand around his waist, pinning his arms to his sides, and one hand across his mouth.

For a moment, we all stare, frozen. The boy wriggles in the brigand's grasp, struggling and terrified. I open my mouth to say something, but I can't think what. My mind won't catch up. Can't compass this next disaster.

"Step away from the caravan," the brigand bellows.

"Easy," Cap says placatingly, and he steps forward, away from me and Karina. He reaches out, arms up, patting at the air like the brigand is a skittish horse.

I scan. Brigands appear behind the man holding Besta. A good dozen, and likely archers up on the hillside as well. "No one needs to get hurt."

Cap's arms are still out. I'm trying to work out whether to pull my blade or not, but my heart hammers hard. Besta. Blessed heavens, not Besta.

And then, before I can react, before any of us can work out what to do, Cap's outstretched hand grasps a throwing blade from the bandolier across my chest. He doesn't even weigh it before he throws, tossing it toward the brigand holding Besta.

The trajectory seems good. My heart is in my mouth. It spins end over end, flashing in the sunlight. Even as it does, I'm reaching behind my shoulder to yank free my sword.

Then the point of the blade buries itself in Besta's chest.

His eyes, pinned to Karina's, shift from terror to emptiness, and my mind falls absolutely, completely silent, lost in observing Besta turn boneless and his body begin to fall.

Karina's scream is piercing. She scrambles forward as the brigand swears and tosses the boy to one side. It cuts through to strike my own heart, and I haul myself together.

I bend to pick up my sword, unknowingly dropped.

"Get your fucking blade out," I spit in Cap's horrified face, my fist bunched in his shirt. It's not even satisfaction to see him pull the blade from its sheath. Bols is pasty-faced, but he too grabs his weapon and spins to face the brigands.

Blade outstretched, I sprint forward and catch the brigand's cudgel in the downward swing that would have ended in Karina's head. She's oblivious to the danger, her entire being focused on the slumped and still body of her child. I shove the brigand back, fury making me fast, spinning to force the point of my blade through his heart.

Karina draws Besta's head into her lap. His body shakes as the last of his life trickles away with the seeping blood covering her knees.

Grief fills my chest, my breaths coming short. These two, this pair, this family... Loss swallows me whole, like a chasm opening beneath my feet. I open my mouth, a keening sound beginning somewhere in the pit of my gut.

No. I can't do this.

I grit my teeth, shove it away. Karina must not die. I cannot let it happen. I let my fury with Cap, my devastation at his killing of Besta, cascade through me, blazing bright and scalding away the freeze.

I turn to face the next brigand coming at us.

As he nears, I cut and feint, duck and turn in a haze, knowing only that I am whirling, dealing death. I'm moving faster than I've known, and somehow, it feels like every strike succeeds, like nothing can touch me. One tries to climb onto the top of a caravan, where Rizzen stands, and I yank him down and plunge my blade through his heart.

When it's done and I am panting, bracing myself upright on my sword, I realize I'm carrying numerous cuts, some deep enough they'll need to be sewn. I felt none of them being laid.

I've killed more men solo in one fight than I ever have before. Seven men lie in a rough circle around me, their blood soaking into the dirt. And at the center of it is Karina, broken-hearted, weeping soundlessly, holding Besta's cooling body. Grief unfurls in my gut again.

Issian and Wens appear from somewhere. They're worn too, and Issian carries a slice to his upper arm. Some part of me notes it'll need stitches.

Tears stream down Wens's face as he takes in Besta and Karina. "Not the lad," he says softly, brokenly. "Besta."

I gulp back my own tears. "I'm so sorry," I mutter, and then turn away before I can see any of their reactions. I cannot bear whatever their response might be—sympathy, commiseration, blame, none of it.

I find the protection crew gathered together around the very first wagon. Rizzen is lookout, on the roof of the caravan that follows it, throwing stars in hands. There are four bodies here. If any have survived, they'll be running by now.

"It was a mistake," Bols says as soon as he sees me, stepping so Cap is behind his shoulder. "He didn't mean to."

I glance down. I still have my bloody blade in my hand, my fingers wrapped around the hilt sticky with coagulated blood. They think I'm coming for him. My fingers tighten. Cutting him down would feel like resolution, I know it. Blood for blood.

"I didn't mean to," Cap repeats. He sounds old. "I... I'm good with a throw."

I stare at him. The desire to swing is strong. So strong. "Good with a throw? Are you fucking kidding me? Even hungover? Even still drunk from last night?"

All I want is to run him through, to pierce his chest just as he pierced Besta's. Let his life trail away as that lad—that sweet lad, that child with a life full of love and laughter before him—had his life taken from him. It's like longing, the muscles in my arm tightening, readying. The breath burns my throat.

But I raise my chin.

My gut is hollow. They drank. I knew it. He ignored intelligence. I knew it. He couldn't keep his crew in line. I knew it.

"You're right. It's not your fault." And I'd said no to Karina so many times. So many times. "It's mine."

I can meet none of their eyes. The grief I'd shoved back fills my chest again, and I can't catch my breath. Tears well in my eyes, helplessness cascading through me. How the fuck did I get here?

No more. None.

The image of Besta's gaze shifting from life to death recurs in my head. The tortuous path that led to him dying—from leaving Picton's troupe, to the swordsman's school, to this—suddenly feels like a crossbow bolt's flight, straight and true. How could I not have seen it?

My sword clanks to the ground before me, my hand gone nerveless. I scrabble numb fingers against the buckle on the harness, promising myself wildly, silent-ly, that I won't put it on again—never again—and let loose a guttural bellow as I fall to my knees. I howl out every skerrick of air there is in me, until I'm panting again, struggling to draw breath, winded by all that's gone.

They stare down at me in silence.

I miss Petrus.

Issian can't even meet my eyes. He glances back, at his feet, at my feet, at my outstretched hand—anywhere but my eyes.

The purse that settles into my hand is weighty, but it's nothing to the guilt. "Thank you," I say, my voice coming as if from far away.

"She can't come out," he says, turning his head away from me. Tears sparkle on his eyelashes, and a suppressed sympathetic sob steals my breath. "Can't do it."

I'd known it would be the case, but it doesn't stop the emptiness of loss tumbling through me. I force a long, slow breath. "That's alright," I say, my voice a croak. "Tell her..." I pause, trying to think of words, but there are no words. None. "Tell her I'm sorry. So, so—" My throat catches. "So sorry."

He jerks his head in a nod and turns away without looking at me. The door bangs against the frame. It's badly fitted and can't close properly.

I swallow, but it doesn't stop the tears. Liza is standing behind me, and I reach out a hand for her warm neck. She turns in toward me, blowing her breath out against my arm—her expression of comfort. It feels like nothing will ever stop these tears, but I know better. I've done this before.

Not killing a kid. That's new. But I've lost my family and my village. I've left Liv, and with her the family I'd found in the troupe. Petrus left me. And now, here I am, enduring yet another loss.

I haul myself into the saddle, raise my head, and tug down my hat. A yank on the reins and we're turning toward the road again. It opens before me beyond the bounds of Tyrasene, dusty and lonely and wild.

I inhale shakily. It's a risk, riding with my blade wrapped in my bedroll on the back of Liza's saddle rather than strapped to my back. Naked. Alone. Exposed.

But I swore it, and the image of the dying light in Besta's eyes hasn't stopped appearing in my mind. I'd best get used to it. Alone is safer. Much safer.

I raise my chin, unshed tears rainbowing the light, and urge Liza forward. I glance back only once at the figure silhouetted in a window of the tav.

I don't even know if it's Karina, but I raise my hand anyway.

Then I settle my gaze on the horizon, where the blue meets the green, and ride on to nowhere.

*Read on to join Des on her next adventure...*

**Excerpt from *The Blood-Born Dragon*,** book 1 of the *Everlands Cycle* below

Release April 2023. Order now: https://books2read.com/u/4j5wQk

## Blurb

**A bond she didn't choose.**

**A love she can't escape.**

**A creature so powerful it bends the limits of time...**

Smart, sassy, and sanguine, Des Mildue is a traveling sellsword in Rescalin, a dry and dusty kingdom full of rogues, opportunists, and thieves. She keeps her nose clean, brazens it out with a blade when she can't, and keeps others at arm's length where they can't mess up her plans.

That is, until a sword fight gone wrong leaves her tied by blood to the first dragon hatched in centuries. Suddenly, Des has to contend with a new voice in her head: haughty, willful Esquidamelion. Des wants to leave Squid by the roadside, but the blood bond has other ideas.

With half the world on their tail - including Liv, her beautiful, faithless ex who Des is *definitely* over - Des must search for answers for why so many are willing to kill, maim and torture to get their hands on Squid. But she's beginning to suspect her blood bond has tied her not only to a dragon, but to a fight for Rescalin's future...

...and no one else even knows it's at risk.

**If you like the kind of story that grabs you by the shirtfront and hauls you through mystery, magic, adventure and betrayal, with a side of sapphic romance, pick up *The Blood-Born Dragon*, first in a new trilogy from debut author J.C. Rycroft.**

### Chapter One

The meaty knuckles swing toward me. I duck too late, the unexpected backhand sending me tumbling from the saddle. I sprawl into red dirt, face pounding. *Ouch.* All I wanted was to get to the next town. I hear they have baths, and fuck knows I reek after crossing this desert. Baths and food and rest. *Beer.* But no.

They're dismounting, laughing. Exchanging witty repartee I can't make out through the ringing in my ear. My cheek is split inside, the blood slick, salt, and copper on my tongue. I spit into the dust. The air smells like heat, and I'll bruise to blues on that hip tomorrow.

I scan the horizon, a red line carved against deep blue sky. It's razor-straight, with no lumpy sign of civilization to flee toward and no one else in sight. Valenta must be an hour or so off yet. Fabulous. To think I managed the whole of this bloody endless red sand without trouble 'til this, and with my blade unhelpfully strapped to Liza's saddle instead of slung on my back.

Well, that one was my choice. My fault.

I sigh, squinting against the sun. They're hefty, and there's three of them. The blade'll help if I can get to it, much as I wanted to not use it. But it's probably not enough on its own. I'm good, but I'm not *that* good.

But there's no one else. So it'll be down to me, then. At least I've had the practice, and Picton always said that's what made the difference when it came to performing. All in. No one for backup. Except Liza, of course—thank all the gods.

Right. *Fuck.*

Any decent swordsman will tell you half the game is in the head, and the best place to play that game is out on the stage.

Still sitting in the road, I level my gaze at them, unveiling the challenge in it. "Really? That's your best offer?" I grin, knowing my teeth are outlined in red. It's only a flicker, but the second-in-command blinks. An iota of fear. I can work with that. I groan and heave myself into a squat.

The leader, a brawny man with a scar carved from eyebrow to chin, grins back. He opens his mouth to speak and glances at his two goons. They always do this—take a moment for their audience. As the goons return his look, smirks dawning, I move. I toss a handful of sand across their faces, kick hard into the leader's belly, and turn immediately to feint left but hit hard on the right with an elbow into the first goon's crotch. He grunts, folds in half, and I stumble as I spin away from the second.

Their mounts panic, kicking up heels and bolting along the road to Valenta. Odd for fighter's mounts, which are usually tempered by many battlefields, but the heavens know I've had to make do with available steeds on a job requiring speed. My mount stands firm, thank fuck. I really don't want to have to walk into a town I barely know when this is over ... assuming I can still walk.

My burst of violence is not going to be enough of a head start. No mercenary or highway brigand would hire backup less than raised to the kill. I need a weapon.

I roll backward through the hard-packed red dirt, sparing a sad thought for my glossy new silk jacket as I spring up next to Liza—the horse they hauled me off. The sword is there, tied into my blankets like only a fool would do. I grab the hilt, and with a swift tug that sends poor Liza skittering sideways and whinnying in protest, it's out of the scabbard.

I grin. It's been a while, but the leather-wrapped, sweat-soaked hilt welcomes my touch like a mother's arms to a prodigal son. Well, not my mother. Then again, I'm not her son. If I'd been a boy, it might've made all the difference. I might've still been in that tiny hamlet herding goats. I might've married and been four kids deep already, not stupidly outnumbered on a desert road, slapping together the performance of my life, for my life.

Making my entrance, I lick the blood off my front teeth and spin the blade casually from hand to hand. A juggler's trick. The bright sunlight glints off the blade. The leader has recovered, as has the first goon. The second-in-command is closer. He'd been coming for me, full of bravado, making up for the stab of fear earlier. But now, he hesitates. Almost there.

*Intensify*, bellows Picton in my memory. *They mustn't be able to look away!* I add an extra half-twist to the juggle of my blade, opening my eyes a little too wide, and the goon glances back at the leader, uncertain.

"Look, I get it," I say, after a decent spell of silence bar the whistle of my sword. "I do. You thought I was easy prey. Here I was, riding along, looking for all the world like a weaponless fool in a pretty silk jacket. You made me an offer based on that assessment. But none of those things are true ... except for the pretty silk jacket."

I pause for a moment, making a show of scanning the desert horizon, blade still spinning in the light. "So why don't we just leave it here? You can go home with all your limbs, and I'll be on my way. Better deal than the one you offered me." The traditional deal of highway brigands everywhere: give us everything and we'll kill you anyway.

Silence. It sounds like a fight coming. I spit on the ground, red on red, and try again. "That can be the measure of blood spilled here. Sum total."

The leader's craggy brow draws even tighter, and his face gets ugly. "So the fucking bitch has a sword," he snarls at his men, his disdain clear. It's always a marvel to me, the way men will loyally follow those who mostly show them contempt. "She's still a fucking bitch. Take her out!"

I'm decent with a sword, but truth be told, I'm a better player. I'd hoped the juggled sword would be enough to at least open negotiations. Wishing for the seven hundredth time that Petrus was still at my back, I sigh, drawing up strength I haven't used like this in a good long while. Time to lean in to what I *do* have.

As the two goons rush me, I duck to cut swift across the middle, then spin right around to cut low, slipping below their blows. I've lost some form since I put my sword away. My breaths grow harsh, the dry air scalding my lungs. Their axes clash against each other above my head, and my ears ring, but they are both bloody across the thighs. I might be a better player than fighter, but that is true of these two, too. They tumble against each other, moaning as long spurts of blood chunk the dirt of the road. They won't be getting up anytime soon, but it won't stop them from screaming at me. I tune them out.

I shuffle back, soft boots stirring up the dust. The leader curses and strides toward me. He raises his blade, and a wily gleam lights in his eye. I meet the sword, eyes on his. We're beyond chatter now.

It's a bit of fancy talk when people compare a sword fight to dance. It's not like any dance I've ever done. My dances are all swaying hips and playing at sex. But then most of those who wax that kind of lyrical about fighting are nobles trying to give it a swanky gloss, and nobles' dances are full of intricate footwork. Really, it's all pretty stories. Sword fights are grim.

The swing is hard, and I wince in anticipation, renewing the grip on my hilt. The blade comes hard against mine. My shoulders complain at the impact, and I grunt aloud, locking my knees for a moment. He thinks where he holds it over me is in strength, and he's not altogether wrong. I shove back panic. Not helpful.

But I've known what looks like weakness on me for a good long while now. I slip sideways, scuffing through sand, and turn my body toward the blade with my own sword for protection, letting his force slide past me, further from where I need him. I slice down his back as I dart backward. He's almost quick enough in his recovery, and the tip of my sword only cuts through the thick leather of his belt. It tumbles about his feet. I grin again, and he grins back.

"Flirting with me, girlie?" he growls, cupping his balls. I almost roll my eyes, but that would mean taking my eyes off him.

"Oh, for fuck's sakes." I feint high and then swing the blade to cut low. They're both feints, really, and he blocks both, but the third move involves a slice across his collarbone, near enough to his face to make him flinch. I want to crow, but he's not there yet. I draw back, knowing he'll be wary now, then shuffle sideways toward him, driving him back, forcing him to turn. Just a little further...

I go for two easy, ugly beginner's swings, moving a bit faster than he can shift that rough, weighty blade, and he's where I want him.

I grin, then yell, "Liza!" The horse raises her head abruptly with a noise of protest—I think she'd been napping—then grumpily points her rear hoof.

He hesitates, glancing sideways at the horse, and I rush in, driving him even closer to her unhappy hindquarters. She tosses her head and kicks back. She doesn't hit him, but she doesn't need to.

He leaps out of the way and into my swing. It's not fancy, but my blade carves through the leather straps holding his vest on and deep into his ribs, curving to tear upward through cartilage, into lung and bloody heart. It hurts my everything—the force of him falling toward me, and holding the sword like this. For a moment, my whole body howls in protest, then I struggle to hang on to my blade as he falls away from it. I stagger back to keep my balance.

"It was a bad deal," I say, almost sad as blood bubbles up to his lips. A hundred times over, this could've been me. It's actually *been* me a good dozen; I've just been luckier with wounds and companions and jobs. His eyes go wild for a moment, then they're still. "You'd've found I'm not disinclined to business, but I'm damned if I'll be fleeced."

"Fucking bitch! You killed him!" A roar from the two standing off to one side makes me look around, assessing.

The road is a mess, blood congealing in the ocher sand. The stink is already starting in the hot sun. This isn't exactly the note I wanted to enter Valenta on—bringing raging bandits in my wake. I don't need this kind of trouble. I need money, and for money, I need work. And for work ... well, since I put away my sword, I've been leaning hard on the Rogue—doing minor theft and sex work, mostly. I can't afford to have this lot telling terrible tales about me, especially to the Rogue King himself.

I swallow, stumble across to catch up the leader's sliced belt with its big, heavy purse, then pause, returning to crouch beside the corpse. He's an ugly bugger, grimy from the road. Probably been a week since he's cleaned his hair.

I narrow my eyes. The blade is better than he is, though, and the sheath has pretty patterns burned into it. Strange combination, but maybe he'd lucked into a new patron, or one of those jobs I used to dream about that pays enough to kit you out forever. Well, luck is one word for it. I can only hope for my sake that whoever sent him wasn't too attached. How is it that since Petrus and I split up, trouble seems to stumble into my path?

I slice the rest of the ties on the front of his vest and yank the two sides back to reveal a small blade tucked into one side—also a bit too fancy for a simple mercenary—and a purse tied tightly to the other. That'd be right. Most traveling swords keep the good stuff close. I myself have a pouch tucked between my breasts with the few things I've kept precious.

The goons roar curses at me. Guess they knew were the good stuff is. I tug the small blade from its sheath, toss them a salute with it, making them bellow even harder, and use it to cut away the purse. It falls open in my hand to reveal three gold coins mixed in with a button, a carved stone, and some sand.

A drop of blood falls from my face into the little collection, and I catch my fist back against my mouth. Still bleeding. I shake my head, and another drop falls. I shove the small purse inside the big one and tuck the blade into my right boot. Waste not, want not.

I glance over toward the two sidekicks as I wipe the blood off my sword on his legs. They snarl curses at me when they see me look their way. They're unlikely to be the forgiving type, and that should mean I kill them now, but it's worth a try. After all, I'm going to be in town first. Maybe I can spin a story that doesn't turn me into some kind of desert-addled demon with a sword. Maybe I happened on the carnage after the fact? After all, who'd be so stupid as to send assistance for men who want them dead?

I shake my head, dismissing the thoughts. Details to be sorted on the road. I go over to pat and calm Liza, shoving the purses into the pouch tied to her saddle horn. "You're such a wonderful girl," I say, smoothing my sweaty hand against her neck, streaking the dirt. "Too wonderful for words." She gives me a look that is half preen and half haughty disgust, and I know I'm forgiven.

I blow out my breath as I untangle the scabbard from the roll and sling the blade across my back, strapping it down. It settles into place easily—too easily—and my mouth tightens. Easy is discomfiting, given the reason I'd put the sword away in the first place. Poor kid. "It wasn't meant to play out like this," I add, as I haul myself into the saddle. "Peaceable was the aim." I reach a finger inside the pouch, reassuring myself about the coin I've just taken. Enough to keep me for a while. Something sharp catches on my finger and I yank it free. "Ow!" I put my fingertip to my mouth, tasting copper yet again.

I unhook my water skin, rinse my mouth clear, and spit. I swallow a good few mouthfuls and toss the skin at the goons' feet. "Gratitude is a virtue, lads." They roar as I leave them behind me in the dirt.

"Not carrying a visible sword was meant to keep us safer!" I mutter as I urge Liza forward. She harrumphs in response as if she could have told me how silly that idea was.

*to be continued...*

## Join the journey!

The best bit about embarking on this publishing thing is that I get to build a relationship with you, dear reader!

My newsletters land about once a month, unless something extra exciting is happening, with details about me, my books, and a short exploration of some of the most intriguing, problematic, and, yep, radical elements of the fantasy genre.

And it's to those subscribed to my newsletter that I first offer all the tasty little treats—deleted scenes (there's a Des/Liv one I can't wait to share with you!), bridging chapters, side stories and other cutting-room-floor tidbits.

Plus, you get the opportunity to join my ARC, beta, and street team!

Sign up now at https://www.jcrycroft.com/newsletter

**Enjoyed this novella? You can make a big difference!**

Reviews are vital to helping me bring my books to the attention of readers who might enjoy them. I'd love to have the connections and, let's be real, financial backing of one of the big five publishers, but I'm a baby indie author.

But I do have you! And that counts for almost everything.

Honest reviews are the best way for me—and you—to invite new readers to join Des on her journey. Well, reviews and word-of-mouth, of course!

Please leave me a review on Amazon or elsewhere if you prefer!

# ACKNOWLEDGMENTS

The list of those I want to thank is long, but as with all of my lists, at the very top is mi novia, Maria, and our righteous babe, Ameyali. Thanks for your super-active support and tolerance of the time I spend in other worlds.

Also to my family-of-origin, especially my mama for reading the things, and my sibs for their thoughts on all things designy. Myf for the pictures throughout, Dan for saving my imprint logo from the horrors of almost-there images. And Demelza and Dad for all the encouragement. I couldn't have got this far without you all!

And to my wonderful friends, for their support and excitement as I took this newest deviation in a life filled with them. Extra thanks to Rosanne for helping me get a website functional for very little $$! So appreciated. And of course to the Rogue Writers, who got to see this MS first and were wonderfully encouraging.

And finally to my swiftly growing team—cover designer Fay Lane, line and copy editor Rachelle Wright, proofreader Nay, and developmental editor, Cameron Montague Taylor—you are all such wonderful people to work with! Fay makes magic out of vagueness, and I am so grateful for it. Rachelle has an eye for detail I love and teaches me all those bits of grammar I should probably have learnt a long time ago, as well as being an excellent foil for my occasional excesses. Plus she's *delighted* by my work, and that is *so* valuable by the time line and copy editing comes around! Thank you so much, Rachelle! And to Nay, whose presence is both ephemeral and ever-present – thank you for finding the terrifying number of typos that find their way into my work.

And many, many thanks to Cee—the first person I didn't already know who I shared work with. Cee manages to balance insight with encouragement, good humor with clear and practical advice, and somehow has such faith that they're excited about my *intentions*, even when the page isn't yet living up to it! I feel very fortunate to have lucked into your guidance on this journey, not least for your alphabet mafia chops, which means I know my characters are going to be safe in your hands (even if they're not in mine).

# ABOUT THE AUTHOR

JC Rycroft is an emerging author of fantasy, living and writing on Wadawur-rung Country in Australia. Their work draws on high and epic fantasy tropes, mixed with a dollop of queer romance, humor, and wit, flawed but fabulous feminist heroes, and diverse-in-all-the-ways characters, liberally sprinkled with philosophical concepts brought to life. She loves bringing together the apparent contradictions: high theory and silliness, profound theoretical concerns with a rollicking good story, and ordinary people with unexpected demands to hero-ism.

You can find JC Rycroft online at:

Facebook: https://www.facebook.com/jcrycroft

TikTok: https://tiktok.com/@jcrycroft

Instagram: https://instagram.com/jcrycroft

Email: contact@jcrycroft.com

# CONTENT NOTE

Alcoholism
Attempted murder
Bullying
Child Death
Cheating
Death
Gore
Homophobia
Hostage
Misogyny
Profanity
Queerphobia
Sex (graphic)
Sex Work
Violence

www.ingramcontent.com/pod-product-compliance
Lightning Source LLC
Chambersburg PA
CBHW010450100726
47904CB00008B/2551